AF271390

BREAKDOWN

A BUGS SULLIVAN THRILLER

DANIEL PYLE

Blood Brothers Publishing
www.bloodbrotherspublishing.com

ISBN: 978-0-9828691-6-1

1 3 5 7 9 10 8 6 4 2

For Mom.
This wouldn't exist if not for you.

They'd been driving less than ten minutes when Bugs Sullivan saw the next rabbit.

"There," he said and pointed to a small yard on the right. "Do you see it? By the birdbath?"

Addie looked away from the road just long enough to follow his pointing finger. "Nope. Nothing." She kept both hands on the wheel and turned her attention immediately back to her driving.

The rabbit sat in the snow, not moving, not looking for food, not doing anything except staring toward the passing car and twitching its nose. Bugs hadn't expected Addie to see it—it had that glow about it, that ethereal wispiness—but he had to ask, had to be sure. The light coming off its fur could have been a reflection from a nearby porch light or the moon. Not *every* rabbit he saw was a harbinger of death.

Addie stopped at a T-junction and asked him which way to go.

"Try right," he said.

She did.

When they'd driven five blocks and Bugs still hadn't seen another rabbit, he told her to stop and turn around. Slowing just enough to keep from skidding on the ice, Addie pulled into a driveway, backed out, and pointed the car in the opposite direction.

That old familiar sense of urgency gnawed at Bugs's belly. He wanted to jump out of the car and run. Find the rabbits. Find the trouble. Help. Except, of course, that was a stupid urge. The car was moving much faster than he ever could have, especially on the icy roads; he would have taken one step, slipped, and fallen flat on his ass. And it was cold outside. And he wasn't wearing a coat. And he wouldn't have gone anywhere without Addie anyway.

"I hate being helpless."

She took one hand off the wheel long enough to pat his thigh. "I know, but you're not exactly helpless."

"Are you kidding? I'm the definition of helpless. Can you imagine me out here all alone?" He rubbed at his stubble and his droopy eyes. "Without you? Without the signs? Running around like a crazy person? They'd have locked me away ten years ago."

She shook her head. "Seven years tops."

He laughed and watched the smile spread across her face. She had a beautiful smile.

"You're not crazy," she said. The car slid on a patch of ice, and she pumped the brakes and eased the steering wheel around until she'd straightened them out.

"Says you."

"Isn't that enough?"

Now *he* patted *her* leg. "More than."

They passed the T-junction going back the other way and Bugs drummed his fingers on the dashboard.

"Come on," he said. "Where are you?" He looked left, right, left again.

"Relax."

He looked at her (or maybe he was glaring, although not intentionally). "Seriously?" The houses they passed were dark, and there weren't any streetlights on this particular stretch of road. He couldn't see much more than the illuminated street ahead and her face glowing in the dim light coming from the dashboard gauges.

"Well, I don't mean lay back and take a nap or anything," she said, "but a few deep breaths couldn't hurt." She pumped the brakes again when they slid on another patch of ice, but she didn't slow down.

"Somebody's dying out there."

"I know."

And, of course, she *did*. He didn't need to tell her that somebody almost certainly *would* die unless they made it there in time to do something about it, that it was up to them and no one else. She knew that too.

He stopped drumming the dashboard, spun his wedding ring on his finger instead. She'd never minded that particular nervous tic.

They topped a small rise and Bugs saw the next rabbit hunkered in the middle of the road. Addie didn't swerve or slow down but drove right toward it. The rabbit stood its ground. Just before they drove through it, Bugs got a good look at its flared nostrils and wobbling whiskers. Its eyes were wide but not scared. If it could talk, Bugs had no doubt it would be saying something along the lines of *hurry hurry hurry hurry hurry.*

"This is the way," he said, and Addie nodded. He looked over his shoulder and saw the animal still crouching on the road, looking over its own shoulder and back at them. When the rabbit disappeared, not into thin air but only into the darkness, Bugs faced forward again.

They drove past more dark houses and through a school zone that probably wouldn't see much action for a few days unless the weather turned and the ice melted. In Connecticut, when he'd been a boy, they hadn't missed school for anything less than a blizzard, but here in the midwest, they didn't have the same budget for snowplows and street salters. It would be at least a day before they cleared the roads. Chances were good that there would be plenty of happy kids and put-out parents come tomorrow.

Addie looked at him, just a quick glance. He made a big show of taking a deep breath.

"There you go," she said and smiled again.

The next rabbit was actually two. The animals sat together on a walkway leading up to an old, Victorian house with a drooping jut of a roof overhanging the porch. This time, Bugs didn't have to force the breath, it came out all on its own, like a sigh.

Two meant they were getting closer. There had been days and nights they'd driven for hours before finding what they were looking for, and Bugs's nerves were always a wreck by the ends of those outings.

Outings? More like missions.

Yes, he guessed that was fair.

This time, it seemed, their mission wasn't going to take them much farther than the edge of town.

"Two more," he said for Addie's benefit.

"Already?"

He nodded.

They drove out of town, through outlying subdivisions. Bugs spotted two more pairs of rabbits, then a group of three, and then half a dozen circled around a bike some careless kid had left out on the front lawn. By the time they reached the river and the bridge leading out of their county and into the next, the animals were everywhere: on the sides of the road, hopping across both lanes, scurrying and crouching and gathering all over the place. They drove through the ghostly things, and although Bugs knew better than to expect the crunch of their bones beneath the wheels (they *had* no bones, not really—they were more like wisps of smoke than living, breathing mammals), he couldn't help but cringe every time one of the animals disappeared beneath the front bumper.

It was always like this at the end. A mob of rabbits. A furry, unnatural *sea* of the things.

"We're here," he said.

"Where. I don't see—"

But then she did, and she slowed.

The car ahead sat on the side of the road, pulled into the breakdown lane but still dangerously close to any traffic that might come sliding by.

She eased in behind the parked car and killed the engine. She left the lights on. Bugs saw the missing rear wheel, the jack holding up the car, the man sitting on the icy ground and fumbling with the spare.

The rabbits had disappeared. They'd done their job, led the two of them here, and now they had gone to wherever it was they went between missions.

"Is this it?" Addie raised her eyebrows and frowned.

Bugs shrugged. "I guess it must be. The rabbits are gone, and I don't see anything else." He wrapped his fingers around the door handle and let himself out of the car, cringing at the frigid air that slithered in and wrapped itself around his neck like a snake. He heard but didn't see Addie getting out through her own door. His eyes never left the man sitting beside the jacked-up corner of the car. The holes in the guy's jeans showed white, hairy flesh beneath. His puffy down coat—at least a size too big—swallowed him. Stubble? He had it. Enough that you might have called it a full-fledged beard. When he looked up at the two of them, Bugs could see the red spiderwebs of vessels in his eyes. *Bloodshot* wasn't a strong enough word.

"Is everything okay," Bugs asked. "You need some help?"

The guy shook his head and looked back toward Addie. Bugs followed his gaze. Addie stood between their car and the stranger's, her arms crossed over her chest but not quite hiding the twin bumps of her jutting nipples. They'd both left the house without grabbing their coats, which had been stupid and very unlike them. They were usually more prepared. Addie shivered and Bugs thought about telling her to get back in the car.

Except she wouldn't do that. She wasn't a sitter-by, which was one of the many reasons he loved her.

"I'm...fine," the stranger said. His voice was raspy, slurred. Bugs wondered how much he'd had to drink. "Why aren' you wearing...coats?"

"They're in the car," Addie lied. "We took them off and cranked the heat up to eleven."

Bugs watched to see if the stranger would smile at this. He didn't.

"Can I call someone for you?" He touched his pants pocket and realized he'd left his phone in the car. Stupid.

The man shook his head again.

"What happened?" Bugs asked. "Nail?"

"I dunno." Which seemed to be all he had to say on the matter. He let loose a sound that was half burp and half cough.

Bugs looked past the stranger, keeping an eye out for an oncoming car or a pack of coyotes, watching for some kind of imminent danger. Of course, the danger might be something else altogether. Maybe the jack would slip and the car would crush the guy. Or maybe there would be a problem with the spare and he'd freeze to death waiting for help. Death was coming for Mr. Tirechanger in one form or another; that was all Bugs knew and all he *needed* to know.

"Why don't you let me take care of that for you," Bugs said. "And then we'll drive you somewhere warm."

"I'm plenty warm," Tirechanger said. "Anybody needs warming up, I'd say...it's Tits over there." He gesticulated toward Addie with a tire iron Bugs hadn't noticed until just that second.

He heard Addie shift. Probably repositioning her arms to cover the body parts in question.

"Let's not—" Bugs started, but before he could finish, something thumped in the back of the stranger's trunk.

"What was that?"

The stranger dropped the tire iron and started to stand.

The thump came again. A single word followed. It was muffled, but Bugs thought it sounded very much like a cry for help.

Or a warning.

He looked at Addie. Her eyes went wide.

"Look out!" she yelled.

Bugs turned just in time to see the man with the bloodshot eyes point a pistol at his head and pull the trigger.

The bullet whizzed past Bugs's ear and ricocheted off something metallic behind him. The car probably, although Bugs didn't turn to look. Nor did he glance back to see if the ricochet had taken a deadly turn toward his wife, although his mind screamed at him to do it, to make sure she was okay.

When someone shoots at you and you don't have a weapon of your own or somewhere to hide, the most important—the *only*—thing you can try to do is get the gun away from the shooter before he or she can pull the trigger again.

Bugs hunched and charged the stranger, screaming, slipping on the ice but able to keep his traction. Barely. White, pluming exhalations slipped out of his mouth and through the cold air around his head. The gunman aimed the pistol, and for one terrifying second, Bugs was looking right down the barrel, but before the loony could squeeze off another shot, Bugs reached him and threw a forearm into his throat.

Bugs hadn't built up a lot of momentum in the short distance between the two of them, but the blow was hard enough to knock the guy back into the snow. Tirechanger landed on his butt and slid across the frozen ground. The gun popped out of his hand, disappeared under the car. He brought his hands up to his Adam's apple, sucked in two short, gurgling breaths, and looked up at Bugs. *Glared* up.

Bugs had almost fallen too. He threw out his arms and just managed to keep himself upright. When he regained his balance, he shuffled and slid his way to the stranger and, before the guy could say or do anything else, kicked him in the face.

The man fell back into the snow, hands still clutching his throat, eyes rolled into the back of his head, a stream of blood running out of his busted nose and over his lips.

The kick had been a vicious thing. Brutal. Bugs had used every bit of strength he had, and it made him nauseous to have to do it, but he'd learned a long time ago that it was stupid and potentially deadly to give an attacker any kind of benefit of the doubt. In Bugs's opinion, if someone shoots at you, he pretty much deserves whatever he gets. If you show him any mercy, you might as well start shooting at yourself.

He leaned over, felt the guy's neck for a pulse, found one, and went to fish the gun out from under the car. When he found it, he tucked the pistol into the waistband of his pants.

Then, finally, he turned back to his wife.

She sat on the ground beside their car, her hand

pressed to the side of her head and a dazed look on her face. She had her knees pulled up to her chest, and she was shivering.

She's shot! Bugs thought. *He shot her in the head. No, God. Please no! Not my Addie.*

Except there was no blood. Or none Bugs could see anyway. And Addie looked more surprised than injured. He hurried over, dropped to his knees beside her, and asked if she was okay.

She took her hand away from her head.

There *was* blood.

But not a lot. Just a trickle running down her ear and a smear on her fingers and palm. She had a tiny furrow in her earlobe and another on her scalp just behind her ear. A lock of her golden hair hung from this second wound, now red and bloody at the roots, looking like it would fall off and blow away any second.

As far as gunshot wounds went, Bugs guessed she couldn't have been much luckier. The bullet had barely grazed her. A light breeze probably would have kept it from hitting her at all.

Or blown it right into her brain.

He shook his head. He wouldn't let himself think those kinds of thoughts. Addie was okay. Bleeding a bit and probably more than just a little freaked out, but okay for the most part.

A gust of cold wind blew into his back, and he winced. The temperature out here was practically arctic, and neither of them had a coat. They needed to get back into the car to warm up.

Aren't you forgetting something?

He stopped.

The thump? That muffled cry. There's someone in that guy's trunk.

Christ. He *had* forgotten. For a second anyway.

"Listen," he said. But before he could tell Addie what she needed to listen to, she glanced over his shoulder and screamed.

Bugs looked back just in time to see the tire iron zipping through the air toward his head.

Then the cold, white world disappeared behind a fog of darkness and agonizing pain.

He found the rabbit in a strip of tall grass behind the garage.

Rabbits, technically. There were four of them. Three dead.

The fourth animal, the survivor, squirmed in the bottom of the grassy depression, looking malnourished and scared. No...terrified.

Will's mom had once told him that if he touched a baby bird, its mother would kill it. Smell the stink of humanity, she'd said. This had been several years earlier, in the summer between first grade and second. Will had never been sure if the warning was the truth or a lie meant to keep him from climbing trees and hunting nests, but he'd decided to stay clear of baby birds anyway. Just to be safe. Now he wondered about the rabbit. If he reached in and touched the bunny, separated it from its dead brothers or sisters, would its mother come back and know? Would she smell the stink of humanity and snuff it out?

He didn't think so. And he didn't guess it mattered anyway. The poor little creature obviously had no mother. Not

17

anymore. No rabbit would have let three of her babies starve to death in a hole. Not if she could help it.

Moving slowly, not wanting to scare the animal more than he had already, he reached into the grass and ran a finger along the rabbit's side. Its ribs—thin, fragile things much too close to the surface—yielded to his touch. He was afraid that if he pressed much harder, he'd break every last one of the bones. The bunny didn't turn its head toward him, but its eye did seem to flick in his direction. Its side hitched arrhythmically as it sucked in ragged breaths.

Dying. It was dying. You could see it clear as day.

"Don't worry," Will said. "I'll help you." Not sure if he could—not sure anyone could—but sure he would try.

He eased his hand under the rabbit and lifted it carefully out of the hole, half afraid it would scratch him or flip out of his grasp and fall to the ground, sure he was doing more harm than good.

But it didn't flip or scratch, and it didn't fall. It seemed to be using every last bit of its strength just to stay alive. And it was scared. Don't forget that. Will guessed he would freak out too if some giant came along and plucked him up.

He carried the animal across the back yard, walking carefully. The last thing he wanted to do was trip and fall and crush the rabbit beneath him. When he pushed through the back door, he called for his mom.

No response.

He carried the bunny into the utility room, found an old shoebox, lined the box with a ratty but clean towel, and laid the animal inside.

Now the rabbit did look up at him. Or seemed to. It twitched its head his way and wiggled its nose.

"Just hold on," he told it. "I'm going to get you some milk."

He wasn't sure if regular milk was good for a rabbit, but it had to be better than nothing. He carried the shoebox into the bathroom, found an old bottle of children's cough medicine (for his little sister, who seemed to get sick at least once a week), and removed the eyedropper.

Or did you call this kind a throatdropper?

Didn't matter.

Will squeezed the dropper into the sink and rinsed it off under the faucet. By the time he'd finished, the rabbit's breathing had started to slow.

"No!" Will said. "Don't die. Please!"

He hurried into the kitchen, grabbed the milk from the fridge, poured some into a coffee mug, and filled the dropper.

The first time he poked the dropper into the animal's mouth, it moved its head back and let the drop of milk fall to the towel beneath it. Will tried again, and this time the rabbit licked the tip of the dropper and swallowed.

Just a tiny bit of milk. But a start.

"That's good," Will said. "Very good."

He picked up the shoebox and the mug of milk and brought them both to his bedroom. He had some nursing to do.

Bugs—it wasn't his real name, not legally, but it was what Addie called him in bed, with nothing between them but a sheen of sweat, and he thought that trumped a piece of paper in a filing cabinet at City Hall—woke without opening his eyes. For just a second, he felt the dying rabbit's ribs and the irregular hitch in its side, saw it there in the makeshift bed he'd made for it, a drop of milk glistening on its whiskers. He thought about the eyedropper and the spot he'd cleared for the shoebox under his bed, and he tried very hard not to think about what had happened next.

Here, now, the sounds of slush splashing against the car's undercarriage drowned out those last few memories and floated him back into reality. He was in a car—lying, not sitting—and his hands were pulled behind him and lashed together with what felt like some kind of thick tape. Probably duct tape.

He opened his eyes.

Tirechanger sat in the driver's seat, hunched over the steering wheel, hands at ten and two, speeding along and squinting through the windshield like an eighty-year-old nursing home escapee. Earlier, Bugs had thought the guy must be drunk, but if he was, he was the best damn drunk driver of all time; he drove the car perfectly straight—unnaturally straight given the icy road conditions. No weaving, no sudden stops or accelerations. If this had been a driving test, the crazy fuck probably would have gotten a perfect score.

Bugs looked away from Tirechanger and over the edge of the seat. Addie lay in the footwell beneath him, eyes wide and full of tears, her upper body squeezed into the depression behind the front seat, her jumbled legs and feet folded into the the twin hollow on the passenger's side. Tirechanger had hog-tied her with loops of duct tape, binding her hands over her belly and securing them to another wad of tape around her ankles with several more lengths of the material. One last silvery strip covered her mouth. When she saw Bugs—alive and awake—some of the fear left her face, but not all of it. Not even most of it.

Bugs felt a warm, sticky patch on the back of his neck. Blood. And there was undoubtedly more of it gluing his hair to his scalp. Plus a mother of a lump he guessed would hurt like hell once his disorientation and adrenaline wore off.

The gun he'd tucked into his waistband was gone.

He leaned closer to Addie.

For a second, the footwell was a hole in the grass behind his old garage, and Addie was a hyperventilating baby bunny.

Bugs shivered and blinked.

She was his wife again. His beautiful, fantastic wife to beat all wives. His best friend. He wanted to tell her everything would be okay, that they'd get out of this, but he had his own strip of tape—slapped across his mouth and the surrounding stubble—and couldn't do anything more than mumble.

He looked deep into her eyes instead, tried to convey some sense of hope. She blinked away another stream of tears and sniffed.

They had to get out of this car as soon as possible. Bugs tried to think. He twisted his wrists, hoping for some slack and finding none. He eyed the front seat, the windows, the doors, looking for escape routes where there were none.

And then red and blue blinking lights streamed through the back windshield and a police siren warbled.

Tirechanger glanced into his rearview and cursed.

For a second, the car sped up.

He's gonna make a run for it.

Bugs braced himself against the seat as well as he could, knowing a high-speed chase in this weather would likely end in a sliding, spinning, flipping, epic crash but unable to do anything except grab feebly at one of the lap belts behind him with his bound hands.

The sounds of crunching tires below intensified. The police siren first went silent, then blooped, and then started up again. Like some kind of warning. *I said pull over and I meant it.*

The car slowed. Maybe Tirechanger had decided not to run after all. Or maybe he'd never planned to in the first place.

But stopping wasn't really an option, was it? As soon as the cop approached the car, he'd see Bugs and Addie. He'd see the duct tape. He'd see the blood. And then it would be game over for Mr. Tirechanger.

Unless...

"He's going to kill him!" Bugs screamed. The words made it all the way to his lips before meeting the duct tape and collapsing in on one another. They came out sounding something like the mumblings of a three-time stroke victim.

"Shut up," Tirechanger said from the front. The slur in his voice was gone, although Bugs didn't know how that could be, how a person could sober up in an instant. Tirechanger didn't turn around (of course not—the cop might see a move like that and wonder who he was talking to), but Bugs could see his eyes in the rearview. The was nothing but seriousness there. He brought the car to a complete stop and parked it. "If either of you make a sound, I'll fuck Tits to death and then blow both your brains out."

As far as threats went—at least in Bugs's experience—that was about par for the course: vulgar and illogical and yet disturbingly effective. Bugs stared at the man's reflected eyes and didn't make a sound. The red and blue lights continued pulsing, but the siren shut off.

Tirechanger peered into the mirror for another moment. Then he unbuckled his seatbelt, looked down at his door, opened it, and climbed out into the snow.

As soon as he'd gone, Bugs wriggled to the edge of the seat and began rubbing the side of his face and mouth against it, trying to work a corner of the duct tape loose.

On the floor, Addie flicked her eyes desperately toward the back of the car.

We have to warn the cop.

Bugs nodded. He thought he felt a bit of the tape pull

free, but when he tried to maneuver into a position to continue working at it, he managed only to press it back into place.

He groaned.

Below, Addie's chest shimmered out of existence. Or at least that was how it looked. Like someone transporting in a Star Trek movie. But it wasn't her disappearing, it was something else *appearing*. And not just something. A rabbit.

The creature phased into place, sitting on its haunches on Addie's belly. It looked up at Bugs, twitched its nose, and then lifted its front paws like a prairie dog.

"Oh shit," Bugs said.

"Ohmm hhnnt," he heard.

Addie followed his eyes. Bugs knew she couldn't see the animal there. Whatever you wanted to call his ability—a sixth-sense, precognition, prophetic capabilities—the rabbits seemed to be simply some sort of associative link between the psychic and visual areas of his brain, his means of channeling the messages. They weren't actual physical manifestations. Still, he and Addie had been married over ten years and had been partners in these insane escapades even longer. She knew what he was seeing even if it *was* only in his head, and she knew exactly what it meant.

Outside, his voice muffled by the glass and carried away by the blowing wind, Tirechanger spoke.

"'swrong, office...er?"

His slur was back, and Bugs understood suddenly that the man had never been drunk at all, that his apparent inebriation had been a ruse, a ploy to keep Bugs and

Addie's guard down. It had worked on the two of them, and Bugs was afraid it might work again.

And if Tirechanger was faking drunkenness again, it meant he had no intention of trying to talk his way out of a ticket. A drunk driver would draw even *more* attention to the car, right? A policeman wouldn't let some wasted degenerate get back in his car and carry on his merry way.

"Sir." The closed window and the storm muffled the policeman's voice as well, but less so. "Please return to your vehicle." Despite the partial muffling, the words were deep, resonant, authoritative.

"Been driving...all day," Tirechanger said. "Gotta stretch—" *buuuuurp* "—the old legs."

"Sir," the officer said again. Bugs imagined him moving his hand to the butt of his gun, but that was probably just wishful thinking. "There's blood on your face. Are you injured?"

"Jush an acci-dent. No big...no biggie."

"Have you been drinking?"

"Everybody's," Tirechanger said, "gotta drink. Gotta drink to...stay alive."

"Have you consumed any alcohol tonight?" the policeman asked.

Bugs tried to twist around, to crane his neck, to see if he could get a glimpse through the window, but the two men outside were standing too far away. His head ached, and trying to contort his body into the proper position to see any farther only intensified the pain. From his position, he could make out a sliver of blowing snow above but nothing else. He looked back down at his wife.

A second rabbit appeared on Addie's lap. It approached the first bunny and nuzzled its neck with the top of its head. Then the two of them looked at Bugs with their wide, innocent eyes.

You have to do something, those eyes said. *You have to help.*

Except what could he do? Screaming might get them all killed, and he couldn't move even if he'd wanted to. And down there in the footwell, Addie was even more helpless. There was nothing either of them could do. Nothing except lie there and wait and hope for the best.

"Sir—" the policeman started.

And that was when the trunk thumped again. A single *whump* that rocked the car, although only slightly.

"Hhhhhmmmmmmmmmp!"

It sounded like a woman's voice. More muffled than the thump even from inside the car. As if someone had screamed through a pillow. Bugs wasn't sure Tirechanger and the cop would hear it at all.

But the cop did. "What was that?" Some of the authority had dropped out of his voice, replaced by a combination of uncertainty and fear. "Sir, I'm going to have to ask you to open—"

And then there was another sound, this one infinitely louder than the thump or the muffled scream. Like a whip crack inches from your ear, or a peal of thunder close enough to shake the ground. Bugs wished he couldn't identify the noise, but he'd heard similar sounds far too often in this crazy series of events he called a life, some of them this very night.

It was a gunshot.

Something smacked the window above Bugs's head. When Bugs looked up, he saw a young man's face pressed against the glass. His flat-brimmed trooper's hat canted back on his head. His eyes and mouth opened wide, the lips squashed against the window, undulating, fish like. His left eyebrow stopped halfway across his left eye, interrupted by a small black hole. Blood oozed from the wound, streamed across his lashes and his eyeball, down his cheek and into his mouth. As the officer fell, blood smeared across the window, leaving behind a viscous, red mess.

When the man's face dropped completely out of view, another replaced it. Tirechanger's. Covered in a new fan of blood. He bared his teeth and glared in at Bugs. Then he stepped back a bit, pointed the gun at the ground, and fired three more shots.

Bugs worked the tape off his mouth. Not that it mattered much anymore.

You can't warn the dead. It was more than just a lesson he'd learned and re-learned over the years. It was practically his mantra.

He looked down into the footwell and whispered, "Are you okay?"

Addie shrugged and then nodded.

"He shot him," he said, although it was probably unnecessary. From the floor, Addie might not have been able to see as much as he had, but he was sure she'd seen and heard enough.

She only nodded, her eyes full of tears. The rabbits on her stomach had disappeared.

"I'm gonna try to wriggle my way up to the window, see what's going on." The unstuck tape flapped against his lips.

Addie threw her head from side to side, her eyes wide now, unblinking.

"It's okay. I'll only peek."

She shook her head again, and he knew she only wanted him to lie back down on the seat—out of sight, out of the line of fire—but he couldn't do that. No more than he could go back in time and warn the trooper to duck. Some things are impossible, others so against your nature that they might as well be.

He squirmed until the top of his head pressed against the door handle. Blinding pain shot through his skull and down into the rest of his body. He hissed and gritted his teeth.

"Mmmh!" Addie tried to lift her head to him.

"I'm okay," he said after short pause.

She dropped her head back to the floor. He stretched his legs partway out and pressed his feet against the opposite door. He thought if he applied just the right amount of force and twisted his head at just the right angle, he might be able to slide himself up far enough to see through the window. If the pain didn't knock him out first.

A quick look was all he needed. He'd never in a million years call what just happened to the trooper a blessing, but it might at least be an opportunity. Tirechanger had a body to deal with now. Maybe he'd leave it right there on the ground, but maybe he'd drag it to the side of the road or back to the patrol car. If he did, the cleanup might give Bugs a few extra seconds to work on an escape.

Taking a deep breath and preparing himself for the inevitable agony, he straightened his legs. His shoulders slid across the back of the seat, his head up the door. He sucked in ragged breaths and squeezed his eyes shut against the throbbing pain, but he didn't pass out. Still pushing against the door and using his hands to grab at the seat as best he could, he managed to get himself into a position where he could see out into the snow.

Although for several long seconds, the snow was *all* he could see. An infinity of plummeting white specks. Then Tirechanger's head slid into view, and Bugs nearly screamed.

Bugs imagined he saw the madman's eyes—those bloodshot, soulless orbs—glaring at him through the glass. In reality, he saw only the back of Tirechanger's head. The man stood facing away from the car, the trooper's feet clutched behind his back, taking small steps through the snow and dragging the patrolman's body across the road, pausing occasionally to get a better grip on the dead man's thick-soled boots.

Bugs expected Tirechanger to stop when he reached the other side of the street and deposit the body there, but even after he'd walked far past what must have been the edge of the asphalt (with all the snowfall, Bugs could only guess at the approximate spot), Tirechanger kept going. He walked and walked until he eventually disappeared into the snowfall.

The pain in Bugs's head flared and he let himself slide back down to the seat.

"Hmmmmmmp!"

The sound came from the trunk, muffled, barely audible.

"Hey," Bugs yelled, "you in the trunk. We're going to try to get out of here, okay? Just hold on."

"Hmmmmm."

"He's dragging the body away," Bugs said to Addie. "*Way* away." He wiggled to the edge of the seat and leaned down toward her. "I'm going to try to pull your tape off, okay? And then I'll flip around so you can free my wrists."

She nodded.

He leaned farther, stretched until his mouth was only inches from hers. She rarely wore perfume, but she had a naturally sweet smell, and even in these circumstances—or maybe *especially* in these circumstances—Bugs couldn't help but take a big whiff.

He grabbed the corner of her tape with his teeth. Tugging on it sent new waves of agony through his head and neck, but he didn't stop until he'd pulled it completely free and dropped it on the floor beside her.

Addie licked her lips and stretched her jaw. "Are you okay?"

"My head is killing me," he said, "but I'll live." Although he didn't want to take his eyes off his wife, he turned on the seat, twisted, and moved his bound wrists toward Addie's face. With the engine off, the car had started to cool. The windows had grown a thin layer of frost and Bugs's exhalations drifted through the air like smoke.

"Can you reach?"

"I'm trying," Addie said. "Can you get a little closer?"

He did his best, bending his arms and contorting his upper body until he was afraid he was going to pull a muscle. Addie's mouth brushed against his arms and then worked at the tape. He felt her tongue and her teeth and her lips moving from his wrists to the backs of his hands.

Bugs didn't want to tell her to hurry—he knew she was going as fast as she could—but he was afraid Tirechanger might be back any second. He listened for footsteps but heard nothing except Addie chewing and the sound of icy snow blasting against the car.

"There," Addie said. "Pull."

Bugs wrenched his wrists apart, felt the remaining tape stretch and rip. With his arms free, he pushed himself up and peeked out the window again.

No Tirechanger. Nothing but pelting whiteness.

"Do you have your phone?"

He shook his head. "Left it in the car like an idiot."

"Me too."

He tore the tape from Addie's wrists and ankles and then leaned over the front seat and scanned the dash-board.

No keys. Tirechanger must have taken them. Of course he had.

Bugs saw movement from the corner of his eye and instinctively dropped.

"Get down," he said. Although he needn't have bothered; still on the floor, Addie was as down as a person could get without a shovel.

Bugs peered over the window sill, slowly, hoping the thickening frost on the glass would hide him from view, ready to drop completely out of sight if Tirechanger looked his way. The madman shuffled through the storm, minus one dead body. He moved not toward Bugs but in the direction of the trooper's cruiser.

"He's taking the cop's car," Bugs said.

"Think he's switching?"

"I doubt it. He's probably just pulling the cruiser off the road somewhere. Trying to buy himself some time."

Addie sat up and rubbed her wrists. Behind them, Tirechanger turned on the cop's headlights. "On the road or off probably won't make much difference in this weather," she said. "I'm sure they have those things lojacked anyway, right?"

Bugs shrugged. "Probably."

As the cruiser pulled around them, Bugs ducked. He waited until the sound of the car's engine disappeared before sitting back up.

"What do we do now?" Addie pulled herself out of the footwell and sat on the seat beside him.

"I don't know. How long do you think we were driving before we stopped."

"Too long," she said. "We can't get back to our car, if that's what you're thinking. Not without coats. Probably not even with them."

Bugs sighed and rubbed his temples.

"We should look for a weapon," Addie said. "Something we can hit him over the head with when he gets back."

Bugs agreed. "But first, the trunk."

"Yeah," Addie said. "What kind of psychotic serial kidnapper are we dealing with here?"

"The worst kind," Bugs said. He wrapped his fingers around the door handle and took a deep breath. "Ready?"

Addie nodded.

Bugs threw the door open. A blast of arctic air blew through the opening and took his breath away. He wanted nothing more than to shut the door and stay inside. Instead, he rushed into the storm and around to the back of the car. Addie got out behind him, went to the driver's door, opened it, and reached for the trunk release.

When the trunk's lid clicked and popped only partway open, Bugs grabbed it and swung it the rest of the way up. Snow swirled all around him, sticking in his hair, feeling great on his pounding head but terrible everywhere else.

He looked into the trunk, gasped, and took a step back.

"What?" Addie said. "What is it? Is she okay?" She moved toward Bugs.

He looked up at his wife and then back down.

The woman in the trunk wasn't a woman at all.

She was a kid.

Even if Bugs hadn't seen the wet spot on the front of the girl's pants, he'd have smelled the odor wafting out of the trunk—smelled it despite the freezing wind billowing across his face—the stink of urine was pungent and unmistakeable.

The duct tape on the kid's face extended beyond the corners of her mouth and disappeared behind the back of her head. It looked like Tirechanger had wrapped it around several times. Tightly. Pulling the stuff off would probably rip away several clumps of her curly brown hair too.

Addie circled the car. When she saw the girl, she gasped and pressed her hands against her mouth. "Oh my god," she mumbled against her fingers.

The girl might have been eight or nine. With her legs doubled up against her chest and the terrified look on her face, it was hard to tell. She could have been even older, but at the moment she looked scared and very *little.* She lay with her back pressed up against a dirty, flat tire. The one the madman had been replacing when they'd found him, Bugs assumed. Tirechanger had taped her wrists together, and she held her clasped hands in front of her face like someone praying. Which might have been exactly what she'd been doing.

Bugs clamped his mouth to keep his teeth from chattering. He knew he and Addie couldn't stay out here in the blizzard much longer. That *none* of them could. The girl must have been coldest of all. The interior of the car had been warm enough, but Bugs doubted if much of the heat had worked its way into the trunk, and now that they'd stopped, whatever vestiges of warmth there might have been were long gone, sucked away forever by the icy storm. Although she wore a thick coat zipped all the way up to her neck, her pants were plain (and rather thin-looking) pajama bottoms, and she wore no shoes. Just a pair of spotted socks as thin as or thinner than the pants. The girl's visible skin looked purple, half frozen.

"It's okay," Bugs said. "We're going to get you out of here."

The girl shook her head and looked more frightened than ever. Her eyes were emerald green, lustrous, and seemed to reflect an unnatural amount of light. Her cheeks and the tip of her nose were rosy, but the color looked more garish than vibrant, like paint on a china doll.

Bugs glanced at Addie, whose skin had taken on a purplish hue of its own.

"It's okay," she agreed, looking at Bugs but talking to the girl. Then she reached into the trunk and started the quick-but-careful work of unwrapping the duct tape.

While she freed the kid, Bugs studied the road, looking in the direction Tirechanger had driven, watching for a shadowy figure heading back their way. Even if they got the girl out of the trunk, what were they supposed to do? They couldn't drive, and it would be suicide to try and walk.

Then again, it would be a different kind of suicide *not* to try, wouldn't it?

Addie hissed sympathetically as a strip of tape and a tuft of hair pulled away from the girl's temple. "I'm so sorry," she said.

The girl only shook her head again.

Bugs scanned the trunk, looking for something inside he could use to defend them when Tirechanger came back. Other than the girl and the flat tire, the trunk held almost nothing. There were a few oily rags in one far corner, a strip of faded paper that might have been a receipt plastered to the carpet by the girl's head, and a few scattered blades of dry grass. Not exactly the makings of an arsenal.

Bugs wondered how this poor creature had stumbled across Tirechanger's path. Was she a relative (in kidnap cases, they often were, or so Bugs had heard), or had Tirechanger picked her out of a crowd, maybe spied her on a sledding hill somewhere, stalked her, abducted her in the night while her parents slept their last solid night's sleep? Had it been more random than that? Maybe Tirechanger had stolen this car to escape some other crime, found her in the back seat and decided to hold on to her in case he needed leverage in a standoff with the cops.

Who knew? The possibilities were limitless, but regardless of how the girl had fallen into the psycho's grasp, Bugs now fully understood why the rabbits had brought him here, understood his mission.

Addie peeled off the last loop of duct tape slowly, wadding it into a ball as she went. Bugs thought removing duct tape probably hurt less if you did it in a single quick motion, like a bandage, but he didn't think the rule applied when the tape was wound up in your hair. Surely losing a few follicles—no matter how drawn out the process—was preferable to having a chunk of scalp jerked out.

Addie leaned farther into the trunk and adjusted her footing. She stood between the ruts the car's tires had made, and the snow came up over her shoes, partway up her shins. Even if they found a way to take Tirechanger down, Bugs wasn't sure how much longer they'd be able to drive in this mess.

And then he had a wonderful thought: maybe Tirechanger had crashed the police cruiser. At this very moment, he could be lying in an icy ditch, reaching feebly for the sky, bones broken and flesh mangled, gasping and turning the snow pink.

If only. It was much more likely that the monster would come strolling back at any second, grinning and whistling. In Bugs's experience, true evil rarely got what it deserved.

They were all three trembling now. If they didn't move soon, chances were good Tirechanger would come back to find them all frozen to death. Whether that would disappoint the kidnapper or tickle his funny bone, Bugs had no idea. He must not have wanted them dead yet or he'd have killed them already, but that didn't mean he'd be sorry to see them go.

You won't get rid of us that easily, Bugs thought. *In fact, you won't be getting rid of us at all. And Mother Nature sure as hell won't do it for you.*

He was convinced they would make it out of this situation alive. Not unscathed—it was already too late for that—but alive, which was good enough. It was a feeling he got sometimes during their missions. Call it part of his ability or simple optimism, but he'd never been wrong. Of course, he'd only get to be wrong the once.

The last length of tape lifted away from the girl's lips with a hiss, and the words came pouring out.

"I heard a gun bang," she said. "Is he dead?" Bugs couldn't tell if she looked excited or worried about the idea.

Addie shook her head. "No, he's not."

"At least not that we know of," Bugs said. "He's just gone. But he could be back any second." He didn't want to scare the girl, but she needed to know the reality of the situation, that time was not on their side.

The girl thought for a second and then said, "You have to leave me here. Please. Close me back in here before he gets back. You can run if you want, but you can't take me." Her lips trembled. Her breath rose from her mouth in drifting white puffs.

"It's okay," Addie said before Bugs could think of

how to respond. "It's okay to be scared, but you don't have to be. We're here to help you. You're safe now."

"No," the girl said and shook her head to emphasize. "I'm not safe and neither are you. He's a bad, bad man."

When Bugs reached into the trunk to undo the tape holding the girl's wrists together, she jerked her hands out of his reach. He raised his own hands in a gesture of surrender.

"I'm not going to hurt you," he said.

"You might not," she said, "but *he* will. You have to go away and leave me alone." And then she squeezed her eyes shut, sobbed, and said, "You don't understand."

"Help us understand," Addie said. "What's your name? How did you get here? Who is that man?"

Tears dripped down the girl's cheeks. She opened her eyes, looked from Bugs to Addie, sniffed, and said, "He's a bad man."

Addie said, "That's for sure. And that's why we have to get you away from him as quick as possible. Get you someplace warm. Call the cops."

Now the girl's eyes went wide. She shook her head back and forth so violently he was afraid she might hurt herself.

"No," she said. "No no no no no. You can't call the policemen. The policemen are his friends."

Bugs looked at Addie, swallowed a lump that felt like an ice cube, and said, "I don't think that's true. He just...uh...hurt a policeman."

The girl continued shaking her head, although a bit

slower now. "Maybe that one wasn't his friend then," she said, "but some of them are."

"How do you know that?" Addie said.

"Because they come to his house," she said. "They eat with him and drink grown up drinks, and...and they help him hurt us."

"Us?" Bugs said. "Who's us?"

"All of us," the girl said. Her pink cheeks and cat's eyes faded for just a moment behind another cloud of silvery breath. "Me and the other kids."

The next day was a Tuesday. In the school cafeteria, when he was sure no one was looking, Will took a carrot from his lunch tray, wrapped it in a napkin, and slid it into his front pocket next to the quarter he'd found at recess. He wasn't sure what his buddies might have thought if they'd seen him do it, what kinds of rumors such an action might have fueled, and he didn't want to find out. He could lie, of course, tell them he was saving the carrot for later, but what kind of kid saves carrots? Or even eats them in the first place? And if they'd called him on it, maybe tried to punch the truth out of him, he might have spilled the beans, told about the rabbit in the box under his bed.

He didn't want to do that.

He hadn't told his mom or his sister. He hadn't even told his best friend, Alex, although he told Alex everything, even the stuff about his dad. He'd have to tell somebody eventually, he knew—probably Alex first—but for right now the rabbit was his secret. Not his only secret, but the only one that made him happy.

After school, he'd closed himself in his room and shaved slivers off the carrot stick with his Swiss army knife. When he slid the rabbit's box out from under the bed and presented the animal with a pile of the shredded veggie, the rabbit sniffed at it but made no attempt to eat.

"I don't know if you're too little to eat this," Will said, "but if not, please try. Okay?" Tomorrow was library day, and he planned to spend the entire period reading up on rabbits and what they liked to eat, but for today, all he had to go on was what he'd seen on TV. Bugs Bunny and Winnie the Pooh's friend Rabbit were always talking about, looking for, or munching on carrots, and although Will knew cartoons sometimes stretched the truth, he wasn't sure why they would lie about something like that.

The bunny rolled an eye toward him, took a slow, shallow breath.

"I'll just leave it there. You should try to eat some if you can, but I'll get you some more milk too." He'd managed to feed the rabbit a couple of droppers full of milk the day before and that morning before school, but he wasn't sure if that was too much, not enough, or just right. He'd thought about asking his mom, even if it meant sharing his secret, but she had enough to worry about.

In the end, the rabbit (he supposed he ought to give it a name, but he couldn't decide on a good one) hadn't eaten any of the carrot, but he had gotten the little guy—girl?—to swallow several more drops of milk. The bunny didn't look any less starved, and it still hadn't moved much, but it hadn't died either, and Will guessed that was about all he could hope for. For now.

He sat there for a long time, stroking the bunny gently—so

gently—between its ears. When it closed its eyes (still breath-ing, only asleep), Will eased the box back under the bed and shut off the lights.

For Will and Alex, library day was all about the drawing. Although the library's art section filled only half a shelf, three of the books in that small bunch were from a series called You Can Draw and gave you step by step instruc-tions on how to sketch everything from simple shapes to com-plex objects like race cars and superheroes shooting lasers from their eyes. They hadn't mastered the superhero yet, but Alex said when they did, they'd draw a whole comic book together. Will thought that sounded awesome, but he was a little less optimistic about their chances of ever being that good.

Walking to school that morning, Will considered ways to tell Alex he couldn't draw without either giving up his secret or making Alex think he didn't want to spend time together. He couldn't think of anything good, but in the end it didn't matter. When he got to the classroom, Alex's seat was emp-ty.

"Home sick with the flu," Mrs. R told him when he asked. "But I'm sure he'll be all better really soon."

No Alex would make reading up on the rabbit a lot easier, but it also meant being best friendless for the whole day. At recess, instead of hunting for treasure or drawing on the sidewalk with rocks like he and Alex sometimes did, he had to play basketball. A fun enough game, maybe, but less so when the captain of your team (Jerry Tharp, that buck-toothed bully) thought you couldn't shoot and refused to ever pass you the ball. At lunch, there was no one to trade food with, which sucked especially hard that day because they were serving peaches—one of Alex's favorite foods, but one that made Will want to barf out a lung.

He'd already decided to call Alex when he got home, see if he thought he'd still be sick the next day. If so, Will might fake a little flu of his own.

But first, the library. When Mrs. R brought them in, Will went immediately to the librarian's desk and asked if she had a book on rabbits. She looked at him the way his mother sometimes did when he'd made an especially big mess, like she was just about annoyed enough to scream. You would think a school librarian would enjoy helping kids find books —it was kind of their only job, right?—and eventually Mrs. Peterson did, but not before some serious grumbling and a murmured word that might have been a cuss.

After retrieving an index card from the catalog, the librarian led him to the nonfiction section, running her finger over the spines of the books, checking their numbers occasionally against the one on the card. When she found what she was looking for, a thick brown volume on the top shelf, she tapped it, nodded, and pulled it down.

"Please return it to the cart when you're finished," she said and handed over the book.

Will thanked her and assured her he would. Then he took the book to the empty table on the other side of the library where he and Alex liked to do their drawing and opened it.

With its big words and lack of pictures, the book wasn't exactly what Will would have called kid friendly. He thought he'd never be able to find what he was looking for.

But he did. Eventually. The chapter was called "Rabbits and Hares" and between information about the average sizes of the animals and the differences between wild and domestic rabbits, he found a section on feeding orphaned babies. As he read, his heart sunk. If he was understanding the book (and he was sure he was—the language was more advanced than he was used to in some places, but it wasn't like it was written in Russian), the bunny needed not only milk but a special blend of ingredients that he had no access to whatsoever, including something called colostrum that sounded like the kind of thing you couldn't possibly get from anywhere other than a specialty store.

Will flipped the book shut and pushed it away. It slid across the table and nearly toppled off the other side.

"Great," he said, and some unseen classmate or teacher shushed him.

He didn't think he had any options left now. If he didn't tell his mom about the rabbit, have her bring him to a pet store for the special things he needed, the baby would die, and a secret rabbit didn't do a whole lot of good if it was also a dead one.

Once he'd told her about the rabbit, there was still a chance she might make him get rid of it, or even kill it, but Will thought it was a slim chance. After she'd seen the animal, maybe petted it a little, he didn't think she'd deny him the chance to try and save it. Especially if he paid for the supplies with his own allowance. He had thirty-two ones rolled up in his sock drawer and nothing else to spend them on.

Remembering the promise he'd made Mrs. Peterson, he retrieved the big brown book from the other side of the table, shuffled to the return cart, and deposited it beside the other books.

From somewhere a few stacks over, he heard Jerry Tharp whisper something that made several other kids laugh. Will doubted it had anything to do with him (have you seen Will the Wiener try to shoot a basketball?), but somehow it still felt like they might be laughing at him.

I heard he carries carrots in his pockets. What a freak.

That's nothing. Someone told me he breeds rabbits under his bed.

Stupid jerk doesn't even have a dad.

Will shook his head. No one over there was talking about him. They'd probably forgotten he ever existed.

According to the clock on the wall above Mrs. Peterson's desk, Will had twenty minutes before Mrs. R rounded them up and herded them back to the classroom. Twenty minutes was plenty of time to pump out a few drawings, but he didn't feel like drawing. Or doing anything else for that matter. Instead, he grabbed the first book he saw—Amazing America: From Its Discovery to Today!—took it to one of the big armchairs near the windows, and pretended to read it while staring out at the trees swaying in the wind.

He and Shelly were supposed to walk home together after school every day. Mom's orders. They occasionally ditched each other if they'd been fighting, but most days they met at the flagpole in front of the school and trekked the two blocks home from there.

Shelly was there that Wednesday, sitting crosslegged on the grass below the fluttering flag and brushing the hair of the doll she sometimes carried around in her backpack.

She was six, what Will and his friends called a kiddie-gartener—as if they hadn't been kiddiegarteners themselves just a few years ago—but sitting there with her doll and her loose pigtails, she looked much younger. Will wasn't sure he'd ever considered his sister's age before. At least not beyond the fact that she was younger and littler than he was. But he did that day, and the memory of it would haunt him for the rest of his life. How young his baby sister had looked. How innocent.

"Hey, Shell."

She looked up, smiled, and shoved her dolly back in her pack.

"Ready to hit the road?"

"What's that mean?" she said and slung her backpack over her shoulders. Questions, questions, questions. Shelley had more of them than a whole room full of teachers.

"It means get going, I guess. Head home." They moved onto the sidewalk. Side by side.

"Why?" Her bright green eyes narrowed. "Hitting the road would hurt your hands."

Will shrugged. "It's just a saying."

"Oh. Well, I think it's a dumb one." She hopped over a crack in the sidewalk and her pigtails flew.

He shrugged again, as if to show he didn't really care what she thought, although secretly he agreed.

When they were nearly at the end of the block, the school bus rolled past, its wheels thumping through a pothole in the road. The kids inside screamed and laughed, and although

Will sometimes wished he could join the riders (especially on those days when it was raining or snowing and cold enough to freeze snot), this was not one of those times. The sun was warm and the breeze cool. Despite his rabbit problem, it was a perfectly fine day for walking.

Shelley skipped the rest of the way home, stopping here and there to look back at Will, either waiting for him to catch up or hoping he'd join her. Fat chance of that. Will wasn't going to risk someone seeing him skipping along the sidewalk with his baby sister. If they did, his basketball skills would be the least of his problems.

When they reached the house, the first thing Will noticed was the car in the driveway. It was too early for Mom to be back (Wednesdays were her long shifts—"8-5 but still alive" was her hump-day motto), and this wasn't their car anyway. Mom drove a rusty old Buick with balding tires and a dent in the driver's side door. The vehicle parked in their driveway now was smaller, and red, and much newer. Maybe brand new.

Will looked beyond the driveway and the little red car to the front door. Someone had opened it. Opened it and left it open. He could see the entryway and part of the living room through the gap.

Shelley looked at him and grinned. "Who is it?"

"I don't know," Will said, not grinning at all. He grabbed Shelley's shoulder and chewed his bottom lip. "You wait here," he said finally. "It could be a stranger."

Shelley's eyes widened. She might only be a kiddiegartener, but she wasn't a dummy. "What are you gonna do?"

And that was the question, wasn't it? If it was a stranger, what could Will do. Run? Scream? Wet his pants? He knew the smart thing to do would be to go somewhere and call 911. They'd learned all about it at school. But what if it wasn't a stranger? What if Mom had gotten a new car and come home early to take them for a ride? The last thing he wanted to do was call the cops on his own mom.

"I'm going to peek through the window," Will said. "If you hear me yell, run across the street to Mrs. Newman's house and call the police. Can you do that?"

She nodded, but her eyes had gotten wider than ever.

"You know the number?"

"Nine one one," she recited. Apparently even the kiddie-garteners had gone to that assembly.

Will looked around and pointed to a nearby bush. "Go hide behind there." He said. "Just in case."

She nodded again and went. When she had disappeared from view, Will approached the house, tiptoeing across the lawn. The nearest window was the one that looked into his own bedroom. He hunched, crept up to it, and then slowly stood until he could see over the sill.

Someone had trashed the room. Torn books lay in piles beneath the bookshelf. Broken action figures, rumpled clothes, and various toys littered the floor. His bedsheets were piled on the bare mattress, covered with feathers from his torn pillow.

Will now knew with one hundred percent certainty that the car was not their mother's. No matter how mad she might have gotten, she never would have done anything like this.

He sucked in a series of long, ragged breaths.

Beside the bed lay an object Will first mistook for a stuffed animal. Only he didn't have any stuffed animals. He'd passed on the few he once owned to Shelley.

The rabbit.

Will pressed his face against the glass. His first crazed thought was that the animal must be dead, that whoever had destroyed his room had found the rabbit and killed it, but then the bunny moved. Just a small twitch of its back legs, like maybe it wanted to get up.

Will pushed on the window, trying to get it open, wanting only to get inside as quickly as possible and make sure the baby rabbit was okay. But the window was locked. Of course it was. Mom came through every night and double checked.

What now? Break the window? No, he couldn't do that without drawing the attention of whoever was inside. Again, he knew the smart thing to do, but the thought of calling the police, leaving the rabbit behind when it might be hurt or even dying, made his stomach churn. He had to try to help if he could. He didn't think he could live with himself otherwise.

He hunched back down and shuffled along the side of the house, staying out of view just in case the stranger glanced out through a window. When he reached the open door, he stopped and waited, taking deep breaths, listening. He heard nothing except his own thumping heartbeat.

When he had decided it was as safe as it was going to get, he took his first step inside, avoiding the creaky floorboard just beyond the door. Two more steps. After each, he paused for what felt like an eternity, listening for movement in the house.

Another step.

Now he could see the full living room through the archway on the right. There, on the couch, lay a man Will hadn't seen in over three years. A man with a face very similar to his own.

His father.

Covered in blood.

And then Will heard the crash from deeper within the house.

"O ther kids?" Bugs looked at Addie, saw his own confusion mirrored on her face, and turned back to the trunk. "What...other kids?" His teeth clicked, lips jittered.

"I don't know...all their names," she said, also stumbling over words, also shaking.

Addie leaned into the trunk. Maybe to get out of the wind, maybe so she wouldn't have to yell so loudly over the storm, maybe only to get closer to the girl. "How many?"

The kid shrugged. "I...don't know. A bunch. He moves us...around sometimes. From house to house." Her lips and cheeks were crisscrossed with red blotches from the duct tape. A single drop of blood welled near her ear, hung there for a moment, and then dribbled to her jaw, leaving a thin streak behind.

Bugs shook his head and glanced at Addie again.

"He...what? Kidnapped you? All of you?" Bugs's teeth chattered nonstop. He wrapped his arms around his chest and rubbed furiously at his biceps and shoulders.

The girl didn't answer for the longest time. She looked from Bugs to Addie, chewing at her lower lip, her emerald eyes glistening. The wad of duct tape lay beside her head. Clumps of her curly hair stuck out of it at odd angles, billowing softly when the wind snuck over the lip of the trunk.

"Not exactly," she said finally, speaking the words through another silvery puff of air. "Some of the others. Most of them. Maybe all of them. But me and my brother...we're...different."

"Brother?" Bugs and Addie said together.

The girl nodded. "He's got my brother. My little brother. At one of the other houses. I haven't seen him in weeks, and now he might be bringing me to him. Finally. That's why you can't take me away. I don't know where any of the houses are, and if I don't go with him now, I might never see my brother again." She shivered, and the last traces of color drained from her face.

Bugs moved beside Addie, put his arm around her, squeezed close so they could share whatever warmth they might have left and form the semblance of a windshield for the girl.

Bugs said, "That's—"

"Unbelievable," Addie said.

The girl huffed. "I knew you wouldn't believe me. Grown ups never believe anything. But—"

"No," Addie said. "I'm sorry. We do believe you. It's just...a lot to take in."

The girl—

No, he couldn't go on thinking of her as *the girl.* "What's your name?" he asked.

"I'm Shelly," she said, and the name left Bugs speechless, breathless.

It was just a coincidence. Had to be. And yet, with everything Bugs had been through in his life, with every new mission the rabbits led him on, he'd found it harder and harder to believe in anything like random chance.

Addie looked at him, eyebrows raised. Then she turned back to the trunk. "My name is Addie, and this is my husband, Bugs."

Shelly laughed. The high-pitched giggle sounded almost eerie given the circumstances. "Bugs? Really?"

Bugs smiled. "That's my name. Don't wear it out."

Addie looked over the car, down the road. "Listen," she said. "We're going to help you save your brother, okay? Him and all the rest of the kids. But we can't just tie you back up and leave you in the trunk. We have to get help."

"What kind of help?"

And that was the question, wasn't it? If what the kid had said was true—and Bugs didn't see any reason not to believe her—if Tirechanger had friends on the police force, cops who not only knew about the kids but actually helped him hurt them,

(And what exactly did that mean? Bugs wasn't sure he wanted to know.)

where could they turn for help? Someone higher up than local police? The FBI? Whether or not these circumstances made the crime a federal offense, Bugs doubted the feds would simply ignore him if he called and told them he'd found a duct-taped girl in the trunk of a car.

But that brought up an even bigger question: even if they wanted to call the FBI, how could they? They had no cell phones, and there were no houses in sight. No buildings of any kind. Just the car, the road, clumps of trees, and a whole world of snow. Other cars might pass. Or they might not. This wasn't a major highway, and it wasn't cruising weather.

For a brief moment, something glowed on the horizon. Maybe headlights, or a bedroom window in a farmhouse otherwise obscured. Or maybe not a light at all but rather something Bugs had only imagined. He'd gotten whacked across the head after all. He reached up and touched the sore spot, felt the blood crusted in his hair. If he had seen something, it was gone now, lost for good in the ever-thickening snowfall.

"This guy," Addie said, "Mr. Crazy. What's *his* name?"

Tirechanger, Bugs thought.

The wind gusted and blew a sheet a snow into their faces. Bugs scrunched his eyes and turned away.

"He ma...makes us call him Sir," Shelly said, "but I've heard the other grown-ups call him

(Will. She's Shelly and he'll be Will.)

Clark."

The name was innocuous enough, nothing that held any special meaning for Bugs, but he thought he'd ignore it all the same. In his mind, the psycho would forever be Tirechanger.

Shelly pulled her legs closer to her chest, and Bugs noticed the pattern on her socks for the first time. The small spots were not actually spots at all but elongated orange cones with fluffy green tops.

They were carrots. Little Shelly wore a pair of carrot socks.

Coincidence.

Random chance.

Yeah right.

"Why would he take us?" Addie said. "Me and my husband. Has he taken other grown-ups before?"

Bugs couldn't believe he hadn't wondered this himself. Why hadn't Mr. Crazy "Clark" Tirechanger gunned the two of them down? He had the weapon and no qualms about cold-blooded murder—the dead patrolman proved that—so why not finish the job?

"Uh huh," Shelly said, shivering nonstop now despite her coat. "Sometimes. He brings them to...help take care of the kids. Clean them...clean them up and stuff. Feed them. He chains them up on real long chains with these big thick handcuffy things on their arms so they can move around but not get away."

Manacles. I think she's talking about manacles.

"And then, after a while, they...go away."

"Go away?" Bugs said, looking up and down the road, expecting a car or an approaching figure any second now. "Go away where?"

"I think..." She closed her eyes. "I think he *kills them.*" She whispered the last two words, and when she opened her eyes, tears spilled down her face.

Addie reached into the trunk, touched the side of the

girl's head. Shelly flinched away at first—perfectly un-derstandable—but then grabbed Addie's arm, pulled herself up, and wrapped her hands around Addie's neck.

"Oh, honey," Addie said. "It's going to be okay. We're going to figure this out, okay?"

Shelly buried her face in Addie's shoulder. Her curls of brown hair billowed in the wind, collecting snow. As she sobbed, her thin body shook, and her cries nearly drowned out the whooshing storm.

"I don't think we have a lot of options here," Bugs told Addie. "We can't walk. Not like this. We'll all freeze to de...we'll all freeze."

Addie looked at him over the top of Shelly's head and nodded.

He'd started to lose feeling in his fingers. He'd always thought of frostbite as something you got trying to scale Everest or hunt yeti, but he knew if they didn't warm up soon, it could become a serious concern. That or hy-pothermia. Or both. Or maybe some other cold-related dangers he wasn't even aware of. "I think we've got to get back in the car. Wait for a better chance to get to a phone or take him by surprise or...something."

Addie's eyes were full of worry, but she nodded again.

"But first," he said, "I want to check the car, see if he left...anything useful."

"A machine gun maybe?" She said. "Or a map with all the places he's keeping these kids circled in bright red marker?"

"You never know." He smiled.

"I don't think we're that lucky." She kept her grip on Shelly, clutching her with one arm and stroking the back of her head with the other.

Bugs said, "I think we're unbelievably lucky most of the time. Just...maybe in ways we don't always understand."

She nodded again, nothing but seriousness in her face now.

He shuffled along the car, tried the passenger's door and found it locked. Watching the road, wondering where Tirechanger had gone, what he was up to, he circled the hood and let himself in through the driver's side.

It was warmer in the car, but not by much. As he crawled in, he checked the floor around the pedals and the console between the footwells. Nothing in either place but a few gum wrappers and a sticky ring in the bottom of one of the cup holders. He scooted across the seat and popped open the glove box.

A few fast food napkins. Loose change. A single leather glove with a ripped seam. A handful of papers, one of which listed the owner of the car as a Lola Simmons. Tirechanger's girlfriend? Wife? Sister? Or just a random stranger whose car he'd stolen?

Bugs would have put his money on the latter.

The glove box held nothing else. He thought about taking the glove. It might not be the height of fashion, but maybe it would keep at least a few of their fingers from freezing off.

But he couldn't risk it. Tirechanger probably wouldn't open the glovebox, or he might open it and not realize anything was missing, but if he *did* open it, and if he *did* notice the missing garment, they'd lose any element of surprise they might have gained. One set of warmish fingers wasn't worth that.

He leaned into the footwell and patted beneath the seats. He found nothing but a few more scraps of trash under the driver's, but his fingers brushed against something else beneath the passenger's, something cylindrical and coiled like a waiting snake. He grabbed a handful of loops and dragged the item out where he could see it.

A set of jumper cables. Frayed in places and worn to the bare metal in others, the oft-used cords looked like they were as likely to start a fire as charge a battery, but Bugs thought they'd do just fine as a means of choking the life out of someone.

Should he ever get the chance.

He pushed the cables back under the seat, shoving them nearly to the rear footwell so he'd have access to them from the back seat if the opportunity arose.

He surveyed the front seats one last time, looking for anything he might have missed. When he was sure there was nothing, he backed out of the car, brushing against the door frame as he exited. The lump on the back of his head throbbed. The pain had continued to grow there, sending roots down his neck and into his shoulders. He'd have given just about anything for a handful of aspirin.

He touched his scalp and checked his finger tips. No fresh blood. That was something at least. He remembered the madman coming at him during that first terrifying encounter, brandishing the tire iron and...

The tire iron.

Bugs smacked his forehead. How could he have been so stupid? He'd completely forgotten about it. Despite a throbbing injury that should have been a constant reminder.

Or perhaps because of it.

Where had Tirechanger put the thing?

Bugs had been unconscious when they left the scene, but he doubted Tirechanger would have left the tool there. Not with a spare that would need removing soon, not when it would be just as easy to toss it into the car.

Except it wasn't in the car. Or not in the passenger compartment anyway.

Bugs closed the driver's door, shutting in the memory of warmth, and circled around the car until he could see past the trunk's open lid.

There stood Addie, holding Shelly to her chest, clutching the back of her head and angling her away from the vehicle, as if to protect her from something.

And there stood Tirechanger, the something in question, grinning wickedly, pointing his gun at Addie's face.

Bugs started to rush him but slid in the snow and fell to the ground instead. Not that it would have mattered. Tirechanger had already swept the gun in Bugs's direction. Had he not slipped, he might have gotten a step or two closer, but he probably would have ended up with an extra orifice for his trouble.

"Watch your step," Tirechanger said. "It's gonna be a slippery one." Then he barked out a short laugh. "I guess next time I'll have to use more duct tape."

Bugs looked up from the snow, spit out a mouthful of the powder. "Go to hell," he said.

Addie gave him a look that was somehow both appreciative and disapproving at once. A wifely look he couldn't have reproduced if he'd practiced for a week.

He saw a sliver of Shelly's face, but the rest stayed buried in Addie's chest.

Tirechanger's mangled nose had swollen significantly, and Bugs wondered if he'd broken it. He couldn't tell for sure, but he thought maybe he had. He certainly *hoped* so.

"Maybe someday," Tirechanger said. "You can keep a seat warm for me." He leveled the gun and pulled back the hammer.

"NOOO!" Addie shrieked, and the ferocity in her voice made even Bugs flinch. Shelly jerked in her arms and buried her face more deeply into her chest.

Tirechanger lowered the gun an inch and turned back to her. "Jesus Christ," he said. "I knew you had a set of lungs on you..." He looked her up and down. Slowly. "And I do mean a set." He laughed. "But that was something else."

Bugs stayed totally motionless. He couldn't follow his own earlier instinct to rush the gunman, not from this position. Any attempt to stand would alert the lunatic long before Bugs could get into a strategic position.

Oh, what he would have given for a gun of his own. A shootout probably would have left them all dead, but at least he'd have gone down shooting. He didn't want to die on his belly. In the snow. With snot and half-melted slush dripping from his face.

"Don't shoot him," Addie said. "Please."

"Why not?"

And that was a question as loaded as the gun, wasn't it? Any answer Addie gave was just as likely to get Bugs killed. With a psychopath like Tirechanger, trying to guess the right response was like trying to guess the winning lottery numbers.

"Because I love him," she said.

Tirechanger laughed. "Everybody loves somebody sometime. Doesn't do me much good." He ran his free hand over his mouth. "How about we make a deal?"

Addie hoisted Shelly, who suddenly looked much bigger than she had in the trunk, repositioned her with a grunt. "What kind of deal?"

Now Tirechanger licked his lips. "How about I spare Twinkle Toes here," he said, "and you show me your very best appreciation."

"I..."

Bugs pushed himself up far enough to nod his head, trying to tell Addie with his eyes that she should agree to anything, that the most important thing right now was to get back into the car. It was the only chance they'd have of getting the upper hand. The jumper cables were still right there under the seat, ripe for the choking.

"I..." Addie said again. She'd either missed Bugs's look or decided to ignore it. "What kind of appreciation?"

Tirechanger wiggled his eyebrows. "The raunchiest kind. The kind that leaves a nice, juicy mess."

Addie wrinkled her nose. Rabbit like, Bugs couldn't help but think.

He doubted she realized she was making the face and hoped Tirechanger didn't notice it.

"That's not going to happen," Addie said.

No! Bugs didn't think he'd ever wished for anything harder than he wished for the power of telepathy right at that moment. *Shut up! Tell him what he wants to hear.*

Tirechanger shrugged. "Sorry, bud," he said. "Guess she doesn't really love you after all." He pointed the gun and pulled the trigger.

Bugs saw Addie scream, but he heard only the thunderous roar of the gunshot. The bullet hit the ground just in front of his face, sending a spray of snowy sludge into his eyes before ricocheting over his head with a whizzing sound that reminded Bugs of a summer wasp.

Bugs flinched, pulled his head into his shoulders.

Tirechanger grinned.

Addie leapt, still holding Shelly with one arm but swinging the other down in a long, arcing, karate-like chop that struck Tirechanger's shoulder and spun him halfway around.

What it didn't do, however, was knock the gun from his hand. He pulled the trigger again—another ear-shattering boom—this time shooting the ground somewhere near Addie's left foot. The puff of snow that rose from the impact disappeared almost instantly in the surrounding snowfall. Addie scurried away. She didn't drop the girl, though Bugs had no idea how she managed to hold on.

"Shit," Tirechanger said. "What the hell was that?" He pointed the gun at Addie's face again. "That was my last warning shot, okay? Try that again and you're dead. All of you."

Addie looked at Bugs.

It's okay, he mouthed to her and jerked his head toward the car, trying to make her understand. Whether she gleaned his meaning or just lost her will to fight Bugs wasn't sure, but she took a small step back, wrapped both hands around the girl again, and nodded her head. "I'm sorry."

"Okay," Tirechanger said. "That's better. Jesus." He lowered the gun but didn't take his finger off the trigger. Snow blew across his face, stuck to his too-large coat. For the first time, Bugs noticed the spray of blood covering much of the psycho's chest and splattered down his jeans.

The cop's blood.

Bugs had a sudden vision of the patrolman's body lying off the road, eyes wide and lifeless, mouth ajar and collecting snow. Just his overactive imagination. He hadn't actually seen it. His supernatural abilities (if you could call them that) were limited to the rabbits. Or always had been anyway.

"Okay. We were talking about a deal," Tirechanger said. "And because I like your feistiness, I'm gonna give you one last chance not to fuck it up."

"I—"

"No no no," Tirechanger said. "Shh shh. Don't talk. You want to save your man here?"

Addie nodded, swaying now, running her hand through Shelly's snow-covered hair.

"Okay then," Tirechanger said. "That's good. That's better than good." He glanced at Bugs and chuckled.

"What we're going to do," he said, "is get back in the car."

Yes. That's it. Let's go.

Tirechanger stepped back and gestured toward the trunk. "Get up," he said to Bugs. "If you can."

Bugs pushed himself to his knees first. The snow had compacted beneath him. His hands slid one way and then back the other when he tried to catch himself, but he did get up. Eventually. Like some kind of newborn animal just learning to walk.

The fronts of his shirt and pants were covered with snow, damp. Every inch of his body shook, and he could feel his basic instincts starting to take control, telling him to find cover, find warmth, get to safety no matter what the cost.

"Excellent," Tirechanger said. "Now, Simon says dance on one foot."

Bugs stared, not sure if the guy was messing with him or really just that crazy.

Tirechanger laughed, and Bugs realized it was both.

"Go to the trunk," he said. "Take out the tire."

What's this? They'd driven this far with the tire. Why take it out now?

But he thought he'd pushed his luck far enough already, so he said nothing. Instead, he moved to the car, taking small, careful steps and keeping his face turned away from the biting wind.

When he dragged the tire out, he saw the tire iron still there on the floor. Its lugged arm looked nice and blunt, and the flat, chiseled bit, though not at all sharp, could probably do plenty of damage. If only they'd thought of it sooner. They might have had time to plan an attack, or at least been prepared to fight back.

The weight of the tire nearly knocked him off balance again, but he managed to stay upright and tossed the flat into the snow as far away as he could manage. Which was only a couple of feet.

Huffing, he reached back into the trunk and grabbed the tire iron.

"Uh uh uh," Tirechanger said. "Don't get cute. Fling that thing out into the snow."

Bugs exhaled and curled his arm to throw.

"AWAY from me," Tirechanger said. "Just in case you had some genius idea. I've got this gun pointed right at your head, and I can shoot the wings off a hummingbird."

Bugs doubted that, but he also didn't think you needed to be an expert marksman to shoot a man from a few feet away. He *knew* you didn't, as a matter of fact.

He tossed the iron just past the tire. It slid for a few feet and disappeared beneath the snow.

Bugs turned back to Tirechanger. Addie and Shelly hadn't moved. The girl hadn't said a thing since Tirechanger got back, and Bugs wondered if maybe she'd slipped into some kind of shock.

"There's no need to put the girl back in the trunk," Bugs said. "As cold as it is out here, and with those tissue-thin pants you've got her dressed in, she's going to freeze." He eyed the place where the tire iron had disappeared, eyed Tirechanger's gun, looking for an opportunity to do *something*.

"Kids love riding in the trunk," Tirechanger said. "It's like a carnival ride. Isn't that right?" He looked at Addie, but they all knew he was speaking to the girl.

Shelly hitched in Addie's arms, maybe startled or maybe sobbing. "Yes, Sir," she said finally without turning her head from Addie's chest. "So much fun. It's all we ever talk about."

Bugs couldn't help but grin at that. The girl had some spunk.

Tirechanger snorted. "You're lucky I'm in a good mood, you little shit."

If this is his good mood, I never want to see him pissed.

"You leave her alone," Addie said.

"That's exactly what I'll do. Just as soon as you. Put. Her. In. The. Trunk." He waved the gun again. "And that's the last time I'm gonna ask."

Addie carried the girl to the car, shuffling slowly through the snow.

"I'm sorry," she told Shelly as she lowered her. "We'll get you out of there soon, okay?

Shelly nodded and disappeared behind the lip of the trunk.

Addie reached for the lid, and Tirechanger said, "Huh uh. You crawl on in there too."

Addie looked back at him, glanced at Bugs.

"No," Bugs said. "Come on. Wrap us up in more duct tape. Turn us into freaking duct-tape mummies if you have to. But if you try to squeeze us all in there together, we'll be bouncing and flailing and elbowing one another in the face. Especially with the roads like they are."

Tirechanger fired the gun, put another round in the ground between Addie's feet.

"Okay," Addie said, showing him her open palms. "Okay. Jesus. I'll get in the trunk. Just cool it with the gun." She nodded to Bugs. "It'll be okay." Then she pulled herself into the trunk, first one leg and then the other. She too disappeared. For the most part. Bugs could see only her knees.

Bugs started to follow her, but Tirechanger held up a hand. "You hold it right there."

Bugs slid to a stop. Tirechanger went to the car, grabbed the lid, and swung it shut.

"Hey," Addie said from inside, and then added something muffled that might have been *what's going on?*

"What are you doing? I'm riding up front?"

This might still all work out after all. Just give me thirty seconds at a stop light with those jumper cables.

"No." Tirechanger said. "I'm not going to kill you, because a deal is a deal, and I'm looking very forward to the other end of this one, but you're not going anywhere else with me. You have a tricky sort of...what do they call it? An aura? Like you're up to something. And I don't like it." He licked his lips. "Not one bit."

"What do you mean?" Bugs said, although he had a terrifying idea he knew. "I'm not going with you, but you're not killing me? You're just going to leave me here?"

Tirechanger nodded smugly.

"In this weather?" Bugs said. "That's the same thing as killing me."

In the trunk, Addie's mumbling had gotten louder. Before long, Bugs knew, she'd be screaming. He tucked his hands into his armpits and tried bouncing to generate some heat.

"No, sir," Tirechanger said. "In fact, it's the exact opposite. One way, I put a bullet through your skull. The other, I leave you right here, breathing, and with your brains on the inside where they belong. What happens after that..." He shrugged. "I can't be responsible for what Mother Nature does. That's between you and her."

Now Addie was screaming. Things like "Leave him alone!" and "Run, Bugs!" Still muffled, but clear enough.

Bugs's shivers became trembles. He imagined himself standing here alone on the road, then walking into the biting wind and blistering snow, and knew he had no other choice.

He rushed Tirechanger.

Tirechanger started to swing the weapon up. Bugs took one long step and then another, managing to keep himself upright despite the slick underlying ice.

Right until the end.

His last step, the one that was supposed to propel him into the other man, slid out from beneath him, leaving him twisting awkwardly through the air well short of his target.

Tirechanger stepped forward. Not slipping himself, of course. The bad guys never do, do they?

This is it. I'm dead.

He waited for the psycho to pull the trigger.

But he didn't.

Instead, Tirechanger swung the butt of the gun like a carpenter trying to drive home a nail. It hit Bugs in the temple, and the sudden agony turned the snow-white world into something even brighter than white, a blinding flash accompanied by the sound of rushing air, a noise that might have been only the wind or might have been the billowing cloak of Death come to take him away.

Bugs fought to open his eyes but eventually realized he wasn't sure his eyes were actually closed. He felt snow against his face, felt it surging up his nostrils and down his throat every time he took a breath. He heard the sound of a car door opening and closing, and then the growl of an engine layered with the angry, tearful screeches of his imprisoned wife. He tasted blood, or a watered-down cocktail of blood and snow. But he saw nothing except that dazzling expanse of whiter than white.

He pushed himself to his knees, rubbed at his face with his half-frozen fingers. Finally, blurred wisps of the world began to float back into focus. He saw the snow first, a steady flickering, like the screen of an old TV between stations, and then he saw twin red spots of illumination that could have been a set of evil eyes but were more likely Tirechanger's glowing brake lights.

When he heard the tires spinning against the ice, he tried to scream out, to let Addie know he was still alive, but when he opened his mouth, the explosion of pain left him unable to speak at all. Instead, he sucked in a breath of frosty air that only intensified the agony, leaving him doubled over, clenching what felt like every muscle in his body.

The tires spun through the slush, sent jets of it spraying out from beneath the bumper and covering Bugs with freezing grime. His whole world was cold now, an over-chilled frostland, all warmth cursed away like something from a children's fairy tale.

He covered his face with his hands, tried to walk into the spray and fell again. When the car finally moved, it slid across the road at an angle and then back across the opposite way. Finally, it straightened and lurched forward.

On his knees again and wiping at his dripping face, Bugs heard Addie (and maybe Shelly too) screaming and thumping the trunk's lid. As his vision cleared, he saw the brake lights first sharpen and then begin to fade into the still-falling snow.

He tried to scream once more, and this time he finally found the ability to let loose a sound, a low, guttural howl that was half pain and half fury.

But it was too late.

As the sky showered its encroaching death upon him, Bugs watched the tire-changing maniac disappear into the night with a trunkful of his soul.

After dinner, Victor moved through the basement and collected the empty trays. The Bad Man had never told them they had to do this, but they'd found out the hard way that if they didn't send up their dirty dishes when they were done, he would send down food in a nasty old mop bucket the next time. Or make them eat it off the floor. Or not give it to them at all.

He also hadn't told them they had to take turns. This they'd decided for themselves. Just as they'd decided to take turns emptying the potty buckets and comforting the really little kids when they woke up crying at night.

Some of the others weren't very good about it. When their turn rolled around, they'd grumble and complain and then grumble some more, but Victor didn't mind. Not really. It was something to do, and when you lived in a basement with no games or toys or TV or anything, it was nice to have something to do.

The twins sat on their bunk, heads together, whispering. When Victor came close, his bare feet slapping gently on the concrete floor, they both shut their mouths and watched him until he'd grabbed their empty trays and moved on.

Wonder what they're up to.

Probably nothing. Probably twin stuff. They were six years old. Or maybe seven now. Though they both had the same green eyes and curly red hair, Neal's hair was cut short while Sam's was long and usually pulled back in a pony tail.

Which made sense. Sam was the girl.

On the next bunk over, Wolf sat on his rumpled blanket with a last bite of sandwich pinched between his fingers. Wolf wasn't the kid's real name, of course, but it was the only one he would give them, and Victor thought no real name could have been more fitting. Wolf had a nasty snarl, a way of looking at you like he was thinking about leaping onto your chest and ripping out your throat. He pushed the last chunk of PB&J past his teeth, chewed, and handed Victor his tray.

Victor thanked him. Wolf said nothing.

He stacked the tray with the others. They were cheap plastic things, like the trays they gave you in the school cafeteria, except these were all different colors and thicknesses, and some were slightly bigger than others so you had to stack them in a specific order or they'd go sliding out of your hands.

You didn't want that. You didn't want to break anything that belonged to The Bad Man.

When he'd finished, he had a pile of eight trays and a stack of eight cups. No napkins. No silverware. No crusts. They weren't allowed to send back the crusts. They'd learned that the hard way too.

He took the dishes to the dumbwaiter at the far end of the room. The other children watched him. Some of them talked to one another while others sat alone on their bunks, not speaking or even really moving.

The dumbwaiter smelled bad and looked worse. There were moldy water marks where liquids had splashed out and pooled, crusty splatters that might have been mud but weren't. Victor tried not to think about how their food came down in the same box they used to send their potty buckets up. The Bad Man had lined the bottom of the dumbwaiter with rows of razor blades, wedged into cracks in the wooden base and reflecting yellowish light from the basement's single bulb.

Victor guessed the blades were in there to keep kids from hopping inside and trying to escape, but he wasn't sure he saw the point. If you really wanted to try it, you could put a tray in first and climb in on top of that. Except why bother? Getting upstairs wasn't the same thing as escaping. It would only get you punished. And probably the rest of the kids along with you.

He pulled the door closed and pressed the doorbell mounted to the wall nearby. You couldn't actually run the dumbwaiter from down here (which was another reason why trying to escape would be stupid). You rang the bell, and somebody upstairs ran the controls.

Who? Victor had no idea. Not at the moment. The Bad Man brought other adults to help him sometimes—although Victor thought these other grown-ups didn't want to be there any more than he and the rest of the kids—and sometimes they came downstairs. Sometimes with medicine. Sometimes with soap and water tubs. Always chained to the walls or to each other or both.

But almost never the same people twice in a row.

Victor didn't know how The Bad Man tricked them into helping him, or where they went when they left. Shelly said she thought he hurt them, or maybe even something worse, and although she would never say what exactly she meant by that, Victor thought he had a pretty good idea.

The dumbwaiter came to life. It clunked first, a deep crunch within the wall, and then it whirred and began its climb. You couldn't see it through the wall of course, but if you listened, you could just about imagine you *were* seeing it—like a superhero with x-ray vision—sliding up into the ceiling. It reached the top, clunked again, and went silent. Unless something out of the ordinary happened, and it rarely did, the dumbwaiter would stay upstairs until morning.

Somewhere in the house, another machine hummed. A familiar, mysterious noise.

Although Wolf, the twins, and Tomas—who was the smallest of all of them and spoke almost no English—sat on top of their blankets, some of the other kids had tucked themselves in. James. Terrie. The new little blonde girl who hadn't said a word to anyone since she arrived a couple of weeks ago.

It wasn't bedtime yet. They had no clock down here, but they always knew when bedtime had come because The Bad Man turned off their light. Or had one of his helpers do it. There was no way to tell who for sure, because they never came down or said anything when they flipped the switch. You had light one second and none the next. And if you weren't in your bed when it happened, you had to find your way in the dark. In the pitch black dark.

Because the basement had no windows. No way to see out into the world. Not even so much as a crack in the wall. Some of the other houses had them. Windows, that was. Small, grimy panes of glass covered with thick steel bars on the inside. But not this one. They called this house The Hole.

And right now, in The Hole, they weren't curling up under their blankets because they were ready to go to bed. They were doing it because they were cold. Or that's what Victor figured anyway. He knew *he* was cold. His bare feet especially. Freezing, in fact. And although he couldn't see outside, he could hear the wind blowing, and another sound like crackling rain.

Snow. It was snowing, and no one had bothered turning up the heat.

He thought about going to the dumbwaiter again, pressing the doorbell a few more times. They'd tried that before, and sometimes it brought down the grownups. But other times it brought down The Bad Man. And the only thing The Bad Man hated more than breaking the rules was getting interrupted. And extra doorbell ringing was both those things rolled up in one.

He could deal with the cold. They *did* have blankets, and he was tough. They were all tough. They had to be.

He walked to his own bunk, pulled back the covers (a

thin, white sheet and a scruffy brown blanket that wasn't much thicker), and crawled beneath them.

As he tucked himself in, he heard someone shuffling across the room. The basement was one big open space. No interior walls. No partitions. Just a few wooden posts that broke up the area a bit but did nothing to actually create separate sections. On one side, the bunks stood head to toe in two rows. The potty buckets (there were four of them—stained plastic pails with their handles removed) lined the wall at the opposite end of the room, along with a single roll of thin toilet paper.

This wall—the bucket wall—was different from the others, which were hard, rough, dark concrete. The bucket wall had a smooth, white surface, something one of the other kids had once told him was called drywall. It was unpainted, and you could see the seams where one panel met up with another. Once upon a time, a kid had tried to dig his way through it. He'd clawed and ripped at the material until he bored a hole all the way through to the other side...where he'd discovered not an escape into the outside world but only more concrete. The Bad Man had patched the wall and taken the digger away. No one had ever seen the kid again.

Victor hadn't witnessed this himself. He'd heard the story from a kid who'd heard it from another kid who'd heard it from another who might have made the whole thing up. But whether or not the story was real, the patch *was*, a physical reminder that any attempt to escape was futile.

The room's only other major features were the dumbwaiter and, of course, the door.

The door was on the bucket wall, between the patched section and the potty pails. It had what sounded like a million locks. You could hear them click and clack into place whenever The Bad Man or any of his helpers closed it up. Most of the kids beat or clawed at it for a few hours the first time they found themselves locked inside—there were scratches and even a few bloodstains to prove it—but eventually they all gave it a rest. It was a thick slab of a door. Really just a part of the wall that sometimes opened. Nothing you could ever hope to get through without permission.

When the door opened, you could see the steep, dark staircase beyond, but when the door was closed, it was easy to believe the stairs had never existed at all, that they were part of some fairy tale your parents told you, that the only thing beyond the door was another block wall or a pit of rusty razor blades.

The shuffler was Neal. He moved across the floor like someone skating on ice, sliding his feet over the concrete, his socks brushing, brushing. Neal called this his potty walk, and it always made his sister giggle. She did so now, covering her mouth with her pale, freckled hands.

Neal's ginger curls bobbed around his head as he moved. When he passed beneath the lightbulb, his head looked—just for a moment—as if it had caught on fire. He skated past the wooden post nearest the buckets and slid to a stop.

Privacy was a thing they all remembered—some more clearly than others—but something they'd had to learn to live without. No walls. No curtain. Not even a shadowy corner in which to do their business. It was an un-spoken rule that they all looked away when anyone was using a potty bucket, and some of them even plugged their ears and sang or hummed to themselves to try and block out the sound. Not that it was always possible to avoid *all* the sounds. Or any of the smells.

Victor turned away with the rest of them now, gave Neal what privacy he could. He studied a spot on the wall (one of the concrete walls, this was), the way nor-mal kids might study clouds in the sky, trying to see pic-tures in the rough, stained material. He saw the things he always saw: the tree with the flock of birds in the branches, the car full of chuckling clowns, the bizarro creature with the head of a man and the body of a Tyrannosaurus rex. And then he saw new patterns: a baseball bat; a robot with a long, wobbly antenna; a grinning boy sledding down a snow-covered hill.

While he watched one image dissolve into another, he heard Neal dropping his shorts, positioning himself on one of the buckets, and letting loose a series of farts, grunts, and squirts.

Victor concentrated on the wall, where the boy in the sled had become a submarine diving through a sea churning with toothy sharks and moaning whales.

Neal grunted and Sam giggled again.

"Sorry about the stink, guys," Neal said, though you could hear the grin in his voice and tell he wasn't. Vic-tor heard him stand and pull his pants back up.

They had no sink down here. No water except what The Bad Man sent in their drinking cups. Except when the strangers came down with the washing bins, of course, but that only happened once every week or so. The fact that they often had to eat without washing their hands was just another of those things Victor tried not to think about.

The light flickered. Victor looked away from the imaginary seascape and toward the bulb.

Is he turning off the lights already? This soon after dinner?

He never had before. They usually had what felt like hours after dinner. It was their story time. Their joke time. Some days they would save bits of their dinner and use them to put together makeshift games of tic-tac-toe or checkers. Some days they would huddle together and talk about ways they might try to escape, always whispering, never knowing if The Bad Man or any of the other grown-ups might somehow be listening.

The light flickered again but eventually returned to full glow.

Neal hadn't moved from the potty area. The rest of the kids had all turned back toward the center of the room. They watched the bulb. Silent.

Victor supposed some particularly cruel adult might be up there jiggling the switch, messing with them, but he didn't think so. The sounds coming from outside had gotten louder, the wind stronger. He thought this was the storm's doing.

Neal said, "I guess—"

And that was when the lights when out. Not a flicker this time but a sudden, total darkness.

One of the smaller kids (James maybe) whined, and someone else shushed him.

They waited. Victor stared toward where he thought the light had been, the afterglow zigzagging through the darkness like a lightning bug. The storm had gotten louder than ever, but the rest of the world had gone quiet. No whirring machinery in the house, no shuffling socks on the concrete, no giggling twin. Just the wind and the snow and the drumming of Victor's heartbeat.

"I think we just lost power," Victor said.

Across the room, Neal said, "Well that's just great. Now how are we supposed to watch TV."

"Shut up," Wolf said, his voice as low and grumbly as ever but also somewhat shaky.

Was Wolf scared? Victor had never heard him scared, had never heard him anything but grumpy and mean.

The last memories of light faded from Victor's vision.

Across the room, a sock brushed the floor. Neal said, "I guess I might as well—" And then the sound of the brushing sock became a quicker sweep, followed by a heavy thump and the splatter of spilled liquid.

Neal had slipped into the buckets.

Nasty.

Victor waited for him to cry out in disgust or pain or both. When he didn't, Victor sat up, letting his sheet and blanket fall to his waist. "Hey," he said. "Are you okay over there?"

Nothing.

"Neal?" This was Sam, her voice softer, more girly than ever.

Neal still did not respond, and when the light flickered back on, stunning Victor with a glow that seemed twice as bright as it had ever been before, they all saw why.

In the dark, Addie screamed until her throat burned, slammed her fists against the trunk until her fingers throbbed, folded her legs up between her body and the lid and strained against it until she was sure she'd broken every bone between her kneecaps and her toes. She imagined Bugs back there in the storm, hurt and cold and alone, and she pushed harder still. Her body trembled. Every breath she took went in through clenched teeth and came out amid a spray of spittle. Finally, she let herself go limp and sobbed.

The trunk was good sized, and Shelly had been keeping to her side of it, but now she scooted closer, wrapped an arm over Addie's stomach. "I'm sorry," the girl said. Only that and nothing more.

Addie hugged her and cried into her mess of curly locks. She knew she should try to get ahold of herself, that she should be reassuring the girl and not blubbering into her hair, but she couldn't. Couldn't do any of it. Couldn't even reassure herself.

It wasn't the first time she and Bugs had gotten separated, of course—once, years ago, she'd spent the better part of two days tied to a tractor in the back of an old barn, and that wasn't even the worst example she could think of off the top of her head—but she didn't remember ever being so scared for him. He might have otherworldly abilities, might be the most amazing person she'd ever known, but he was still just a man, susceptible to the same dangers as anyone else. Like blizzards. Like head wounds. Like two-ton vehicles slipping across icy blacktop.

The car bumped along, tossing them from side to side like unsecured luggage. The muffled sound of the thrumming engine barely reached them, but the noise coming from the tires was clear and ever present. A wet hiss. A water moccasin.

They rode like that for a long time, arms wrapped around each other, sharing what warmth they had left. Addie felt the car turn occasionally and stop only once for what must have been a red light. If there were other vehicles, she couldn't hear them beyond the sounds of the car and the storm and their own rustling. She didn't quit crying entirely, but she did manage to bring the level down to a heavy sniffle. The trunk smelled of oil and rubber and Shelly's accident, but there was something else deep within the girl's nest of hair: a faint whiff of soap. A memory of cleanliness. Addie concentrated on that.

Okay, that's fine. You've had a good cry, and no one can blame you for that, but you've got to concentrate now. Bugs isn't getting any warmer back there. You've got to do something.

But what? She had no phone. No weapon. No anything.

She knew what you were supposed to do if someone threw you in the trunk of his car: break out a taillight, hope a cop noticed, pray for the best. But given what the girl had told them, at least some of the police might be co-conspirators rather than potential saviors. And even if they got a good one, there was a fifty-fifty chance Mr. Crazy would murder the poor SOB (or DOB). Probably better than fifty-fifty.

She couldn't risk it. Not yet. Not until she had more information.

The car came to another slow stop. Addie wiped at her damp eyes.

"I think we're almost there," Shelly whispered.

"Wh—"

Shelly cupped a hand over Addie's mouth. Her fingers smelled faintly of peanut butter and dirt. "Shh. Listen."

Addie did. She heard the car's idling engine, Shelly's soft breathing, her own beating heart, and—

clink raaaaasssssssssp

"Did you hear that?"

Addie nodded. "What is it?"

"I don't know, but I've heard it before. Right before we get to The Hole."

"The Hole?"

Shelly nodded, her hair sweeping across Addie's cheek. Addie could make out only the faintest outline of the girl's face. Dark was dark, and eyes could only adjust so far.

clink raaaaassssssssp

Like someone swinging a chain against the ground, dragging it through the dirt.

Except there was no dirt here. Or none not covered by growing blankets of snow anyway.

The car jerked forward, and Addie's head went with it. Mouth first. Right into Shelly's face. The girl cried out, and Addie felt warm blood pouring over her own teeth and down her throat.

"Are you okay?" Addie said, gurgling the words. She heard more than saw the girl soldier-crawl away, back to her side of the trunk.

"Got me right in the head," she said finally. "Oww." And then the sounds of furious rubbing.

"I'm sorry."

"I'm okay," she said, sounding very *not* okay.

Addie wanted out of this trunk. Now. Wherever Mr. Crazy was taking them, whatever The Hole was, Addie knew it wasn't anywhere she wanted to be, nor anywhere a kid like Shelly belonged. Or any other kid for that matter.

Me and the other kids.

She pressed a hand to her lips, tried to stop the bleeding. She had a feeling tonight's real trials were just getting started. And here she was without her partner.

There was one bright side, if you could call it such a thing, one faint hint of a silver lining, one thing she knew that Mr. Crazy didn't: he'd taken...

the wrong spouse.
Except "wrong" wasn't a word that belonged in the same sentence as his Addie. Or the same universe for that matter.

Tirechanger had *left* the wrong spouse.

Yes, Bugs liked that much better.

Still, though Addie was smart and brave and beautiful and wonderful in a million other ways, Bugs had one attribute she didn't, and it sat in front of him right now, nose twitching, ethereal body flickering as the snow fell through it.

"Thanks for getting m-me into this mess," Bugs said and wiped the last of the tire-flung slush from his face. "I hope they have a s-special hutch for you in B-Bunny Hell."

The rabbit stared at him and said nothing. They always said nothing, and thank god for that. If the day ever came that they started talking back, Bugs thought he'd skip the psych eval and march himself straight into a rubber room.

"We h-have to f-find Addie," he said. Although of course the creature already knew that. Knew because it was, in some way, a part of him.

The rabbit turned and hopped away. Bugs saw it, just barely—whether by moonlight filtered through the storm, some other natural atmospheric phenomenon, or some very *un*natural psychic bond—but if it got more than a few jumps away, Bugs feared he'd lose it in the surrounding darkness. He pinched his shaking hands between his arms and his ribs, hunched his shoulders, and followed.

He expected the animal to continue up the road, and it did for what felt like maybe a quarter of a mile, but then it turned abruptly and led him off at an angle. To a dilapidated barbed-wire fence that ran alongside the road. To a gap in the fence where the rusty old wire had either been cut or snapped. The land beyond darkened from the white around Bugs's feet to a black abyss not far ahead. He might have been walking into a small back yard or a hundred empty acres of farmland.

Bugs looked back at the road, back in the direction Tirechanger had fled. Every instinct but one told him to turn around, to stick to the road, to do what any normal, sane person would do, but that one (always that one) was more powerful than all the others put together.

Squinting through the snow, Bugs saw no trees, no other fences or structures, nothing but a flat white plain broken occasionally by a low drift. Like a sheet on a poorly made bed. The rabbit led him around one of the mounds to a depression in the land where a second creature sat. The new bunny looked at the first, then at

Bugs, and then in the opposite direction, farther into the distance.

Bugs waited several seconds for the animal to move. When it didn't, he gestured forward with a trembling hand. "Come on. You guys might not freeze to death out here, but I will."

Although he wasn't sure that was entirely true. If he died, surely they'd go with him, right? Yes, unless he'd spent most of his life severely misunderstanding his ability, they'd all float away with his final exhalation.

The rabbits moved—finally—not in sync but each with its own distinctive gait. Bugs had often marveled at how unique they each were. If they'd come in times of peace and quiet rather than stress and chaos, he would have loved to watch them more closely, to learn more about them. Unfortunately, it was a little hard to focus when there were bullets buzzing over your head or buildings on fire around you or machete-wielding maniacs chasing you through the woods.

Or when you found yourself trudging through a blizzard with no coat and no phone. And no wife.

Bugs couldn't tell how far beyond the road they'd walked. When he looked back, he saw nothing but the same monotone landscape that lay ahead. Snow spilled down the sides of his sneakers, soaking his socks and numbing everything beyond his ankles.

Why hadn't he worn snow boots? He couldn't remember ever having been so utterly unprepared. They'd left in a hurry, but that was no excuse. They *always* left in a hurry. He'd been stupid—that's all it was. He wouldn't let it happen again...if there *was* an again.

His legs felt awkward, unattached, like stilts. If he didn't get out of the cold soon, he thought he might lose the ability to walk altogether.

A third rabbit appeared ahead, not sitting but already moving in the same direction they'd been heading. Bugs liked its hustle.

Then a fourth animal joined them from the left, hopping in from the encircling darkness, sporting a pirate's patch of black fur over one eye. Bugs felt a surge of energy. Four rabbits this close together meant they must not be far from their destination.

Please let that be true. Please get me back to Addie.

Something rippled ahead. Not a shape really, but the vague indication of one. Bugs followed the rabbits (there were five of them now, though he hadn't noticed the newcomer's arrival) until the ghostly non-shape became a post-and-rail fence. Not barbed wire this time. Wood. Warped and covered in snow. Three more rabbits sat on the rail straight ahead. Another half dozen congregated in the snow below.

Bugs looked up and down the fencerow as far as he could see, but other than the bunnies, he saw only the fence itself, separating one patch of snow from another equally featureless patch. The rabbits nearest the fence first hopped in place and then moved beyond the barrier into the field on the other side.

"O-k-kay, I g-get it," Bugs said, "but I don't s-see—"

But then he did. In the distance, two lights bobbed and flickered.

"C-car."

The field beyond the fence was no field at all. It was a

road. Covered in snow, unrecognizable, but a road all the same. Unless someone had taken a very wrong turn off the highway.

If anyone else had driven this way, it had been long ago. There was no trace of previous tire tracks.

The lights grew larger and more distinct, but slowly. Bugs shuffled toward the fence and hoisted himself over it with the claws of ice he'd once called hands.

The rabbits faded away one by one, the last just before the sound of the engine finally pushed its way through the storm. Bugs hurried to where he guessed the middle of the road might be, waving his hands and yelling a stuttery word that might have been "help."

The vehicle drew closer. It wasn't a car but a truck, an old pickup with dents and dings indicative of years of heavy use. It slowed, headed right for him, and took a solid thirty seconds to come to a complete stop. For a moment, Bugs worried it might slide into him. After all he'd lived through, wouldn't that be just the most perfectly ridiculous way to go?

The driver's door opened and a figure leaned out.

"Gdn!"

Bugs held his arm in front of his face, shielding his eyes from the headlights. "What?"

"GET! IN!"

He lurched through the snow, circled the front of the truck, and tried to wrap his useless fingers around the passenger-side door handle. After three failed attempts to work it, the door finally popped open on its own. Through the window, Bugs spied the person in the cab leaning over the seat, arm extended.

He scurried into the pickup and nearly screamed when the wave of hot air washed over him. Images of hot glass shattering beneath cool tap water and snowmen puddling under a hot winter sun looped through his mind. He thought that could be him any second, that the human body surely wasn't made to withstand such extreme temperature fluctuations.

"...doing...here..." the burly woman in the driver's seat was saying, but Bugs caught almost none of it. He focused his attention entirely on the gloriously warm air blasting out of the dashboard vents. He pressed his curled, shaking hands right up against them.

Don't forget the glass, he thought. *The snowmen.* But screw it, right? Maybe speeding along the warm-up was the smartest thing to do. He was no scientist. He knew only that the heat felt like a wave of pure heaven.

"Th-thank you." Bugs said.

The driver hadn't slipped the truck out of park, hadn't done anything but sit there and stare at him.

"I'm Gladys," she said.

Bugs introduced himself, and she surprised him by not making a joke or an are-you-serious face.

"What are you doing out here in this weather?" she said instead. Her eyes were big, wide set, coppery brown. Wisps of silver hair curled around the brim of her hand-knit wool cap. A pink and yellow butterfly embroidered on the front seemed to flap its wings as she spoke.

"It's a l-long story."

"I guess it would have to be. Here." She removed the butterfly cap, brushed the snow from his hair with long, liver-spotted fingers, and jammed the hat down on his head.

"No," Bugs said and turned fully toward her for the first time. Her dense bob of gray hair looked thicker even than the cap she'd just removed, and there was something about her mouth (the deep laugh lines maybe) that reminded him of his mother's mother, Granny Ilene. "You don't h-have to do—"

"Shush," she said and slipped the thick parka off her large frame. She was thick rather than overweight (mostly anyway), about as frail looking as a young Schwarzenegger.

"Really," he said, "You don't—"

"I said 'shush.'" She wrapped the coat around his back and helped him get his arms through the sleeves. The garment smelled of hay and cinnamon. "I'm perfectly toasty and you're frozen half to death."

Bugs's hands still shook, but the shaking had slowed. He felt warmth creeping back into his body bit by bit, a sensation that was both painful and joyous. "Thank you," he said and blew into his cupped hands. "Do you have a phone?"

She smiled, and there was Granny Ilene again. Definitely the laugh lines. "Of course."

"Could I borrow it please?"

"Oh," she said, and away went the smile. "I'm sorry. I meant I have one at home. My children bought me one of those e-phone thingies you kids all have, but I could never remember to charge it."

Bugs tried to remember the last time someone had called him a kid and couldn't.

"I have to help my wife," he said. "She's in serious trouble."

He expected a never-ending series of inane questions. It was, in his experience, how most people responded to such a statement. Instead, Gladys surprised him again by asking the only question that really mattered: "Which way?"

Bugs scanned the road ahead, saw the first of the rabbits in the glow of the truck's headlights, and pointed forward.

His finger didn't shake a bit.

Neal sat in a puddle of liquid nightmares.

Mismatched, mud-colored clumps floated in the foul pool as it oozed away from the overturned buckets. Some of the mess had splashed onto Neal's chest and across his stunned face. It dripped from his eyebrows, down his flushed, freckled cheeks...and out of his open mouth.

Some kids gasped. Others groaned. Wolf said a curse word Victor wouldn't have repeated, and Victor, sitting up on his bunk now, clamped his hands over his own mouth to try and keep from barfing.

He succeeded. Barely.

Neal, on the other hand...he looked down at himself, spat out a mouthful of gooey waste, and then unloaded what seemed like an endless stream of puke. Chunks of sandwich and other unidentifiable globs of half-digested food cascaded into the sewage between his legs, running between his feet, sticking to his thighs, splattering back across his upper body and face.

Cries of "gross" and "stop" and *dios mio* filled the basement. Sam got off her bed and hurried toward Neal, but she stopped a foot shy of the muck and wrapped her arms around her belly, maybe trying to hold back her own dinner. As the doubly disgusting pool continued to expand, she retreated one shaky step at a time.

When Neal had hurled himself dry, he wiped his mouth with the back of his grimy hand and cried.

Victor watched the approaching puddle, wondered if it would reach the beds and what they would do about it if it did. Or even if it didn't. They had no water down here, nothing to clean the spillage but the single roll of toilet paper now sitting in the middle of the sludge, looking like it had probably already absorbed as much slop as it ever would.

Sam leaned toward Neal with one hand outstretched, as if she wanted to go to him but couldn't quite make herself do it. Neal, still crying, pushed himself off his bottom and attempted to get to his feet. He managed to stand upright for almost a full second before his socks slipped in the slime and he fell back into the disaster. Face first.

More groans from the onlookers.

Now Neal screamed and scrambled out of the filth on his hands and knees, never minding the liquid splashing all around him or the layer of gunk covering the entire front half of his body. As he half crawled, half slid to his bunk, his sister scurried out of his way. And Victor didn't blame her a bit. Neal looked less like her brother now than The Creature from the Black Lagoon. Victor expected her to shout out something like "Stay back!" But she said nothing.

None of them said anything. They watched in shocked disbelief as Neal yanked the thin blanket from his bed and used it in a frantic attempt to scrub the mess from his face and hair.

Neal didn't clean the filth off so much as spread it around. Rather than utilize every clean bit of the blanket, he rubbed the same soiled section across himself over and over and over, his clenched fists gripping the material so tightly Victor thought he would surely rip it. Each pass smeared the crud around in sickening new patterns.

Some of that is my poop, Victor thought. *That's my poop on his* face.

Since falling into The Bad Man's clutches, he'd had to learn to accept a lot of hard truths, but he couldn't quite wrap his head around this one.

Neal eventually gave up and dropped the blanket at his feet. His eyes were red and wet. His shoulders rose and fell as he sucked in and blew out one heavy breath after another. He looked like he might start screaming any second, but instead, he glanced around at the rest of them and said, "If anybody has a secret stash of wet wipes, now's the time to come clean."

He wiped his eyes and smiled, perhaps realizing he'd said something funnier than he'd intended.

"Get it?" he said. "Come—"

And then the lights went off again.

No warning this time. No flickering bulb. Just sudden darkness.

Darkness and quiet. The humming machinery deep within the house—the furnace or water heater or whatever it was—faded and left only the sounds of the storm outside and the whimpering children in.

Victor thought of the spreading pool of waste, imagined it creeping toward him in the darkness. The liquid became a grinning boogey man, a creature that could reach over the edge of his bunk, grab him by the ankle and pull him into itself, drown him within its putrid depths.

He pulled his knees to his chest, wrapped his arms around them.

"I'm scared," someone said, and it took Victor several seconds to convince himself he hadn't whispered the words himself.

Outside, the storm intensified. Wind howled. Icy snowfall rattled against the house. Once upon a time, he and Shelly would have watched through the big curtained window in the bedroom they'd shared, huddled together under a thick quilt, praying for a snow day. No, for a whole *week* of snow days. A snow month!

But now...could life really take such unbelievable turns? From quilts and snow days to bad men and potty buckets? It didn't seem real. It definitely didn't seem fair.

He heard something creak. Someone's bed. And then the power returned.

The single bulb illuminated the rows of beds and the children huddled in them. Neal had climbed onto his bunk and lay curled there. He'd ruined his sheet and probably the mattress beneath, and Victor wondered again how they were possibly supposed to clean any of this, but before he could consider it any further, he noticed something new at the end of the room.

On the far wall, where the line of pails had stood so neatly until Neal's disaster of a bathroom break, within the splattered mess dripping down the drywall, two tiny, surprised faces stared out from a small plastic rectangle.

The outlet.

Victor had forgotten it was there. It had been so long since he'd plugged anything in that the idea seemed almost fantastical, like magic. And this outlet in particular was as magical as they came, because the topmost face—like a cave-dwelling, wizard-battling, village-scorching dragon—was breathing fire.

Smoke drifted from the semicircular mouth; the mismatched eyes sparked. The wetted outlet hissed and crackled and then popped as the cover first blackened and then began to warp.

"Oh no," Victor whispered.

Flames flickered from the receptacle. Waves of orange and blue curled up the wall beneath thickening black smoke.

Sam screamed, and somewhere behind Victor, one of the other children said, "Fire," in a voice so emotionless it scared Victor nearly as much as the flames themselves.

The fire climbed, halfway to the ceiling already, charring the wall as it went. Smoke billowed across the joists, thick and dark and coming their way.

Victor hopped off his bed. He didn't consider himself especially brave—in a comic book, he might have been a sidekick at best—but he didn't want to die, and he knew if he didn't do something about the fire double quick, that's exactly what would happen.

But what? They weren't in a school or an orphanage. They didn't have a fire extinguisher or a sprinkler system or even a window to crawl out of. The Bad Man's basement-jail didn't even have a source of water (unless you counted tears). Victor supposed he could have thrown the pails of potty on the fire if they hadn't spilled, but he had no idea if that would have worked even if it had been possible.

He could think of only one option.

He jerked the blanket off his mattress (his pillow flew into the air and landed in the middle of the bed with a soft *whhhp*) and ran across the basement, ignoring the mess on the floor, splashing through it in his bare feet like a regular kid might splash through muddy water, focusing all his attention on not gagging, not slipping, not stopping. Despite the fluttering flames now only inches from the ceiling. Despite the cloud of sooty air swirling all around him.

Maybe he was a little brave after all. Maybe even more than a little. But there wasn't time to think about that. There wasn't time to think at all. Act. Move. Go.

He skidded through the last of the muck, inhaled a mouthful of foul air and coughed it back out, and wrapped two corners of his blanket around his trembling hands.

The fire churned. The speed with which it had engulfed the wall was unreal. Heat washed back across Victor's face and hands, reminding him ever so briefly of a day millions of years ago when he'd fallen asleep on the beach and earned the worst sunburn of his life. Pre basement, this had been, of course, pre Bad Man, when there'd been beaches and fresh air and big, beautiful skies.

Behind him, the kids were saying...something, shouting things that must have been words but registered only as noise.

Victor held his breath, trying not to suck in any more smoke, and swung the blanket at the wall.

The fire shrank away momentarily when the billowing material flapped against it; then it surged back into place, hotter than ever. Victor turned his head away, coughed so hard he thought something in his throat might have torn, and swung again.

This time, rather than retreating, the fire seemed to grab at the blanket, pulling it into itself, embracing it. One of the blanket's upper corners caught fire and Victor dropped the bedding with a screech.

He doubled over, coughing uncontrollably now. Undulating smoke stung his eyes, twisted through his hair and his clothes, up his nostrils. He scurried away from the wall and the smoldering blanket, knowing he should crawl but unable to convince himself to plop down in the sewage.

In case of fire, get low and get out. They'd learned it at school. There'd been a whole assembly with real life firemen and a spotted dog. The firefighters had decorated the door to the janitor's closet with fake, Crayola fire and taught them how to feel knobs, not panic, get low, and, most importantly, follow their escape plan.

There had been much talk about escape plans that

day. They'd gone back to their classroom after the assembly and discussed it for a good fifteen minutes, planned out what they'd do in case of an actual, honest-to-god fire.

An escape plan. The idea was nothing but a cruel joke now.

Victor splashed through the last of Neal's spill and scuttled between the rows of beds. Two of the smaller children, Tomas and James, had crawled beneath their bunks and lay there crying. Wolf sat on the floor, arms crossed over his chest, glaring at the fire, his eyes red from either smoke or tears and dancing with reflected firelight; he'd never looked so terrifying. Neal lay still on his soiled bed. They all looked at Victor; he'd never felt like such a failure.

Across the room, the fire blazed. It had spread vertically to the overhead joists and horizontally to the thick, locked door. The ceiling all but disappeared within the swelling smoke.

"I'm sorry," Victor said. "I—"

"It was a good try," Sam said. She looked at her brother and then back at Victor. "What do we do now?"

They waited for an answer. From him. As if he was anything but just one of them, just another kid. He covered his face with his hands and told them he didn't know, told them he wasn't sure—

Except suddenly he *did* know. It was the only option left. He uncovered his face, blinked, and told them all to get on the ground. "Stay as low as possible," he said. "I'm going to try something."

Several kids followed his instructions immediately—for a

wonder, Wolf was one of them. The others followed soon after. Once they were all safely on the floor, watching the fire, watching Victor, he backed away, turned, and shuffled to the dumbwaiter, trying to stay as low as possible himself.

He coughed incessantly now. His vision blurred. He wasn't sure he could make it all the way to the doorbell, or that he'd be able to find it in the smoke if he did. When his thumb actually touched the small, circular button, he thought he must be dreaming it, that he'd surely passed out halfway there.

Dream or not, he couldn't quit now. He pressed the button. Hard. And he waited. And he prayed.

Would The Bad Man or one of his helpers come down to punish them? If they opened the door (those long-ago firemen had taught Victor and his classmates never to do this, that opening the door was the absolute *worst* thing you could do), would the fire surge and cook them all to a crisp?

And then Victor had an even more terrible thought: why hadn't The Bad Man come down already? Surely he knew about the fire, right? At least some of the smoke had to have made its way up through the floor, through the vents or the walls or whatever. Right? Victor didn't hear any blaring smoke alarms, but that didn't mean someone up there didn't *know*. What if whoever had been upstairs had already fled the house? What if Victor and the other kids were all alone here in The Hole? All alone in a locked, burning basement?

No way to know. Pointless to guess. This was their only chance, their only escape plan, and all he could do now was hope for the best.

Nothing moved upstairs. Victor heard only the sizzling fire and, beyond it, the faint pattering of the ongoing snow. The dumbwaiter's door swam before him. Left. Right. Back and forth.

He pressed the button again, holding it down for what must have been five or ten full seconds. Behind him, children coughed and wept. He listened for footsteps on the stairs, the clicking and clacking of disengaging locks.

Instead, he heard machinery whirring to life overhead. Something in the wall *clonked* and the dumbwaiter descended.

Of all the possible scenarios he'd imagined, this hadn't been one. The helpers weren't supposed to lower the dumbwaiter after dinner, and The Bad Man never would have. Not in a million years. Not ringing the doorbell after dinner was one of the rules. Clearly defined. Punishable by...well, you couldn't really know, could you? Whatever fresh new horrible repercussions the guy had dreamed up.

Victor wondered if this might be some kind of trick. A test. But whether it was or wasn't, he couldn't ignore the opportunity. The dumbwaiter slid further down, maybe halfway there now.

Don't forget the razor blades. Victor bit his lip and glanced back into the room. Through the smoke, he saw the beds, the children all flat on their bellies, and the overturned potty buckets.

Again, no real choice.

He hurried back into the smoke, back into Neal's mess, his bare feet slipping through the chunky sludge, and fished out two of the pails.

Now he could see almost nothing. Clutching the buckets' rims, he rubbed at his eyes with the backs of his hands, but that only made things worse. He didn't think he had much time left before he'd used up the room's last few wisps of clean air. He staggered back to the dumbwaiter, listened to it scrape down the shaft and then eventually, after what seemed like a lifetime of slow-motion movement, thump to the bottom.

He threw open the door, expecting some horrible surprise, some final kick in the metaphorical teeth, but the dumbwaiter was empty except for the blades wedged in its floor. They glimmered in the flickering firelight. Smoke poured through the opening, filling the space almost instantly. Victor knew crawling in there was a bad idea, but it was also the

(no choice no choice no choice)

only idea. The escape plan. *Stay low. Get out.*

After placing the buckets on the razor blades, he turned back to the other children. "Stay down," he said. "I'll come back as fast as I can. I promise."

Then he took a deep, disgusting breath and climbed in. He had to crouch to fit, one foot in each of the slimy pails, but he *did* fit. After reaching through the opening and slapping his hand against the doorbell, he closed the door and waited.

And waited. Eyes closed. Mouth closed. Not breathing.

Finally, when he didn't think he could hold his breath for even a second longer, the dumbwaiter moved. The sudden, jerky ascension unsteadied him. He fell against the back panel, fingernails scraping the sidewalls as he tried to catch himself, and coughed out his last semi-clean breath. When he inhaled again, the air tasted like pure soot. He gagged, spat the air back out, and sucked in another mouthful even worse than the last.

As the dumbwaiter clambered up, Victor opened his bloodshot eyes and clutched at his throat. Less than halfway to freedom, he slumped forward, his face flattened against the dumbwaiter's door, his small chest completely still. The smoke swirled through the small, enclosed area, looking for its own way out and finding nothing.

The house stank of medicine and barf. Heavy on the barf.

Will wrinkled his nose.

The man on the couch hissed, and Will saw what might have been recognition in his eyes, along with plenty of confusion and pain. He held a wad of bloody material—a towel or an old t-shirt maybe—to his neck. Blood dripped between his fingers. As he sucked in ragged breath after ragged breath, his sunken, almost skeletal face twisted. Spit seeped from his mouth and over the patches of beard growing haphazardly across his cheek.

Will had trouble forming a coherent thought. He knew only one thing for sure: when his mother saw the blood on the sofa, she was going to have a cow.

"Dad?"

Something clattered in the kitchen. Will couldn't see it from here, but he recognized the unmistakable sound of dishes clanging against one another. His father coughed, spat a wad of bloody phlegm on the floor, and said nothing, but someone did respond—the person in the kitchen, presumably, speaking in a voice both gruff and unsteady: "Wh-at? I'm coming. H-old on."

The urge to run grew stronger. Will's mother had given him clear instructions on what to do should he ever see his dad again: hurry straight to a phone and call the police. Tell them about the retraining order. He wasn't entirely clear on what a retraining order was but knew it meant his father wasn't supposed to talk to him or his sister or his mom ever again. Wasn't even supposed to come near them.

But he couldn't run to a phone. Because he couldn't move. Because how could you move when your legs were made of solid lead?

More dishes clinked in the kitchen. Cabinet doors opened and slammed shut.

Will wasn't sure he would have run even if his legs had worked. When someone's bleeding in front of you, you want to help. Or at least Will did. And despite everything, this particular bleeder was still his daddy.

He took a step forward.

His father held out the hand clutching the bloody material—definitely a t-shirt, Will saw now, and not just any t-shirt but his t-shirt, the Transformers tee he'd picked out for the first day of school—but whether he meant to beckon Will or warn him away, Will couldn't be sure.

With the shirt out of the way, you could see the wound—a long, jagged gash that curved up his father's neck from his Adam's apple to his jaw. Blood didn't spurt from the injury the way it did in the late-night movies Will's mom didn't know he sometimes watched, but it did leak out in an alarmingly steady stream. His father's skin seemed to pale by the second. Will could see veins pulsing in his forehead.

Heavy, irregular footsteps approached, and a shadow slid into the living room from the connecting doorway. Its owner stumbled forward with an item in each hand: a metal box Will first mistook for a lunch box but then recognized as the first aid kit his mother kept under the kitchen sink...and a gun.

"Couldn't find any booze," he said, "but there's—"

He caught sight of Will halfway to the sofa and froze. Stopped talking, stopped walking, maybe even stopped breathing. Will couldn't say for sure. He heard only his own manic heartbeat, saw only the weapon clutched in the stranger's meaty fist.

The gun moved, barrel rising, dark muzzle pointing toward Will like an empty eye socket.

His father made a sound. It could have been the word "no" or just a grunt of agony. He had pressed the sopping Transformers tee back against his neck.

"Who the hell's this little punk?" The stranger had droopy, bloodshot eyes, a double chin verging on triple, and a belly that reminded Will of an over-filled water balloon.

Will wanted to say something tough, something like Never mind who I am. This is my house. Who the hell are you? but he could only stand silently as the gun centered on his face and a stream of urine dribbled down his inner thigh.

For a moment, Will was sure the gun would be the last thing he ever saw, that he would die here in the living room in a puddle of his own juices and his tombstone would read HIS FATHER DISOBEYED THE RETRAINING ORDER, but then he saw something else: a flicker of motion in the shadows beneath the sofa.

A tiny head emerged from its hiding spot, turtle like, its small nose twitching.

The bunny.

Except...no...that wasn't possible. Was it? Will had just seen the rabbit on his bedroom floor on the other side of the house. It seemed like an eternity had passed since then, but it couldn't have been more than a minute ago, and the bunny had barely been able to move. It couldn't have dragged itself all the way to the sofa. Could it?

And never mind the fact that to do so, it would have needed to move right past the spot where Will stood, He certainly would have noticed that.

No, not possible. And yet, here it was, appearing out of nowhere, a real-life magic trick.

The bunny moved farther out of the depths, exposing its too-thin, erratically pulsing torso.

Will reached out, and the gesture matched the one his father had made almost exactly, except Will knew what it meant this time: stop, stay back, don't come out here, there's a man with a gun!

Said weapon didn't move, but the man holding it did shift his attention to the floor.

"What're you look-ing at?"

"Don't hurt it," Will said. "Please."

The big man blinked, and then the gun did move. It was just a wobble—maybe a tremor of the hand or a simple read-justment—but in Will's mind, he saw the weapon swing toward the bunny, saw the stranger's finger squeeze the trigger and a bullet explode from the muzzle, saw the shot hit home and the grotesque aftermath.

He dove for the rabbit, his sneakers squelching as he launched himself from the puddle of urine.

And the gun did fire, but not at the bunny. The bullet

whizzed through the air where Will's head had been only an instant before. Will didn't hear it, of course; he heard only the BOOM of exploding gunpowder. The acrid stench of it filled the room. And then he heard nothing but the ringing in his ears.

He bellyflopped just shy of the sofa and reached his hands out to cover the baby rabbit, but instead of meeting the creature's fur, Will's fingers went right through.

Once, many years ago, his mom had dragged a dusty projector down from the attic to show them old home videos—his father had been there then as well, both in reality and in the reels—and at some point during the laughter-filled presentation, Will had reached his hand into the light beaming from the clicking machine and seen the images flowing around his wiggling fingers.

This was like that. The rabbit moved around his hand, but there was no rabbit. Not really. Or not one he could feel anyway. When he waved one hand from side to side, the animal poofed out of existence. Now you see it, now you don't. Abracadabra.

He turned his hands, locked beneath them, peeked under the couch, glanced up at the bloody arm dangling over the edge of the cushions and across the floor at the stranger's grungy sneakers, not expecting the rabbit to re-appear but also unable to bring himself to expect anything else. Reality is a thick blanket you hide beneath, and when you discover a tear in the fabric, you might be tempted not to look through.

The big man lowered the gun.

"I...I didn't..." The words were muffled, half lost within the residual ringing.

Still lying on the floor, Will wrenched his head back to stare up at the man's face. The guy looked not at Will or his dad but back across the room, at the spot Will had just vacated. He looked like a kid who's done something very wrong and knows he'll spend the next recess inside cleaning off chalkboards.

He dropped the first-aid kit. It struck the floor and popped open, spraying medical supplies in a long fan most of the way across the room. "No."

Will didn't hear the word so much as see the shape of it on the man's lips.

The stranger jammed the gun in the waistband of his jeans, grimaced, and scurried to the sofa. He didn't look strong enough to lift much more than a cheeseburger, but in a feat Will wouldn't have believed if he hadn't seen it, the guy wrapped his arms around Will's father, pulled him up off the cushions, and flung him over his shoulder. Never once did he look in Will's direction. He huffed out of the room, shoes sliding through the spilled Band-Aids, ointment, and gauze.

Will's father did look back. There was pain on his face, and something else that might have been regret or sorrow, but Will couldn't decipher the wide range of emotions. Not then and not later either, no matter how many times he thought back on that day. The Transformers t-shirt slipped out of his father's hand and hit the floor with a muffled splat.

The big man lumbered through the kitchen doorway and out of sight. The ringing in Will's ears hadn't stopped, but it had dulled enough that he could hear the back door swing open and bang against the kitchen wall.

It didn't close. A ray of backyard sunlight spilled across the linoleum, the bloody shirt, and the living room carpet.

Will pushed himself into a sitting position, lost in a daze of adrenaline, confusion, and relief.

He looked back, saw the puddle he'd made on the floor and—just a few feet beyond—his little sister.

Shelly stood in the entryway, hands swaying in the air before her befuddled face. Blood dripped from her tiny fingers and from the hole in the middle of her t-shirt. One of her shoes had come untied; the lace lay curled in the pool of blood between her feet, and for one utterly mindless moment, Will wanted to yell at her to tie it before she tripped. She looked from her hands to Will, opened her mouth, and fell back through the doorway.

The rest of that day passed in a blur. There were screeching neighbors and frantic phone calls, a fire truck and an ambulance and policemen asking questions he couldn't answer. There was his mother shaking him and screaming and then his mother again, clutching him to her chest and bawling. At some point, someone must have grabbed him a clean pair of pants, because he no longer felt wet down there, but he couldn't remember putting them on. He had blood under his fingernails, but he didn't know whose. Someone gave him a candy bar and he ate two large bites before scrambling into a bathroom he didn't recognize and barfing out what felt like a lifetime's worth of food he couldn't remember eating.

"You have to get some rest," someone said.

Someone else said, "It's going to be okay."

"There's a reason for everything."

"It's not your fault."

"Your momma's gonna need you now."

"I'm so, so sorry," they all said.

He slept a few fitful hours on a sofa in someone's basement and dreamed he'd transformed into his father. He woke covered in sweat and clutched frantically at his neck, feeling for the wound, before finally turning his face into the musty pillow and crying himself back to sleep.

He didn't return home until the next day. Someone had draped a quilt over the sofa. The congregating adults (some of them he knew, and many he didn't) gave him a plate of food-like mush and sent him to his room.

The grown-ups needed to talk.

Will didn't mind. He had nothing to say to most of them, and there was absolutely no way he could sit there pretending the living room was still just an ordinary room.

He tossed the plate on his dresser and shuffled into the landfill that had once been his sanctuary. Ruined books and mangled toys lay scattered across the floor. The roll of dollar bills he'd kept hidden in his sock drawer was gone. The model T-rex he'd spent nearly a week assembling and painstakingly painting might as well have been hit by a meteor. His favorite jammies lay in torn strips beside the bed.

Beside the bed.

He saw the tiny ball of fur there and couldn't bring himself to approach it.

Please be okay, he thought. Please.

But he knew even before he knelt beside it that the bunny was not okay. It didn't move. Its eyes were glossy, lifeless. He slid his hand beneath it and picked up not a warm, squirming creature but a cold, stiff nothing.

He wanted to cry—he knew he should—but he had no tears left.

"You tried to warn me," he said.

Although even then, some part of him knew that he'd really tried to warn himself.

"I'm so, so sorry."

He wrapped the animal reverently in the shredded pajamas.

Later, when he heard car doors in the driveway and adults milling aimlessly about once again, he snuck through the house and into the back yard. He placed the shrouded bunny in the shallow depression where he'd first found it (its brothers and sisters were gone, snatched up by some hungry animal maybe) and used a trowel from the garage to pile dirt atop it.

He wanted to say something, like they do in the movies, but could think of nothing. In the end, he patted the last of the dirt into place and sat silently before the small mound. He discovered he hadn't run out of tears after all.

When his mom found him still sitting there some time later, she sat down beside him and put an arm around his shoulders. She didn't ask what he was doing and he didn't tell her. They stayed there together for what felt like a very long time, and then she helped him to his feet and told him it was time to go.

Dwayne had seen many strange things in his mid-length life—some real, others...chemically influenced. There had been the man walking a opossum on a leash (real), the indoor fireworks at Madison Square Garden (LSD), the finger in the French fries at McDonald's (real, he thought, although he'd never been able to prove it, even to himself), and of course the man with the extra face (that one had been 'shrooms, which he hadn't touched again since), but he'd never seen a wall of smoke give birth to a child.

He'd been sitting at the table in the dim, grungy kitchen, the chain rattling between his cuffed ankles and against the heavy-duty ring securing it—and him—to the floor. On the other side of the room, a small black-and-white television flickered. He watched but couldn't listen. The pharmacist (as Dwayne had come to think of the man who'd lured him here) had left the machine running on mute and just out of reach. As some sort of punishment, he supposed. Although punishment for what, he had no idea.

He raked his fingernails down his arm, leaving long, red scratches from his scrawny wrist to the scarred pincushion of flesh in the bend of his elbow. Sweat dripped down his face, through the irregular patches of stubble on his cheeks and chin. It had been nearly twenty-four hours since his last fix, but the pharmacist had promised another taste when he returned. Another taste if Dwayne did everything the man asked. And he had. To a T.

Outside, howling wind blew sheet upon sheet of sleet against the house. This Dwayne could hear but not see. Someone—presumably the pharmacist himself—had boarded over the room's only window.

Across the room, Agents Mulder and Scully ran across the screen, fleeing some half-seen menace—him with his coifed 'do, her with her bouncing goodies—and Dwayne rooted for them. On TV, you could get away.

He propped his head up with a cupped hand, elbow pressed into the table's chipped Formica top.

The pharmacist would be back soon. Any minute even. Back and thankful for all Dwayne's hard work.

Any second.

More sweat dribbled down his face. Despite what sounded like downright arctic conditions outside, the kitchen seemed to be heating up by the second.

If you can't stand the heat, get out of the kitchen.

Har har.

It was just withdrawal. He understood that. His *want* mutating into an agonizing *need*. And he knew it would all be better soon, but there was a big difference between knowing a thing and believing it.

I want to believe.

He ran his fingers through his damp hair, massaged his throbbing temples, pressed his tongue against his teeth to make sure they were still there.

In normal circumstances, there would have been nothing remarkable about the dumbwaiter's buzzer. It looked down on the room from the wall above the mechanism's sliding door, a small red box with a flashing light, a device that might have been a fire alarm in another life. If you'd been across the house or watching TV with the sound cranked up to a reasonable level, you might barely have heard it. But here and now, the thing's sudden warble could have been an air-raid siren.

Dwayne slid halfway out of his chair and glared up at the flashing indicator.

What were the little shits up to now?

He looked from the buzzer to the sliding panel and chewed his lip.

They weren't supposed to call for the dumbwaiter— the doorbell was only meant to be a signal to bring the contraption back up.

The buzzer sounded again, screeching at him for a good ten seconds this time. On the screen, Scully leaned against a concrete wall, breathing heavily and clutching her gun.

No one had told him what to do in a situation like this, but Dwayne had always prided himself on his ability to deal. And really, what choice did he have? He could send the little quasi elevator down and see what happened next or he could ignore it and hope the brats stopped interrupting his show.

What would Mulder do?

He stood, dragged his chain across the kitchen, and activated the dumbwaiter.

A motor whirred within the wall as the car descended. Although he'd run the dumbwaiter dozens of times in the days since making his deal with the pharmacist, Dwayne still hadn't gotten used to the thing. The grinding, clanking noises it made reminded him of multi-car pileups and broken garbage disposals, misused machines doing things they'd never been designed to do.

As always, when the car reached the basement, it thumped to a stop. The motor, uncalibrated and surely on its last leg (gear?), let out a final, agonized squeal.

Dwayne returned to his chair and waited.

What if the pharmacist punished him for this too? What if, instead of cutting off the sound to the TV, he cut off Dwayne's supply?

No, He couldn't do that. They'd made a deal. Shook on it even. Like two regular guys.

Dwayne watched the little red box. Watched and watched and watched. The chain jangled between his shuffling, tapping feet. When the doorbell finally buzzed again, he jumped up and activated the lifting mechanism. Maybe he would get in trouble and maybe he wouldn't. Only one way to find out.

The car climbed toward the kitchen, and the sounds it made coming back up were the same ones it had made going down, only in reverse. Nothing unexpected about that. The surprise came when the door opened and a cloud of thick, dark smoke billowed into the kitchen.

And the bigger surprise, the thing he might not have believed even if he'd been under the influence of those infamous 'shrooms? That would be when the soot-covered kid with buckets for feet slid limply from the opening like a deformed newborn from a demonic womb.

"Jesus Christ."

The kid's body slapped the linoleum. One bucket popped off his foot and skittered across the room, coming to rest against the far cabinets. More smoke snaked its way out of the shaft, squeezing past the edges of the car and twisting toward the kitchen ceiling, looking almost cosmic in the TV's undulating light.

Fire. Dwayne didn't understand how, but the house must be on fire.

On the floor, the kid wasn't moving. Wasn't even breathing as far as Dwayne could tell. He scurried over to the small, limp form, knelt, and put a hand on the boy's shoulder.

"Kid? Hey, kid."

He flipped the boy onto his back, leaned his head close, listened for breath, for any signs of life.

"Kid?"

He didn't know CPR, or mouth to mouth, or whatever it was you were supposed to do in a situation like this, so instead he did the only thing he *did* know: he smacked the kid's face. Once. Twice. Half a dozen times. Each slap more forceful than the last. Kept smacking until he could see the imprint of his thin, junky's fingers on the little guy's ash-grimed cheeks.

He'd just about decided the boy must be unconscious or dead when the kid's lips parted and he sucked in a long gulp of air. Dwayne wrapped a hand under the boy's neck and lifted him into a sitting position.

"Breathe," he said. "Come on, man."

And the kid did. He breathed, and he coughed, and he looked up at Dwayne with wild, confused eyes.

Dwayne cupped his hand under the boy's chin and tilted his face up. "What's on fire?"

The kid twisted his head out of Dwayne's hand, spat a wad of charcoal-veined phlegm on the floor, and said, "Everything."

Dwayne stood, pulled the boy to his feet, waited to be sure he couldn't fall back to the floor, and said, "We have to get out of here."

The kid laughed, and it was the strangest sound Dwayne had ever heard. Completely joyless.

"No duh," he said and kicked the second bucket across the room.

As he watched more smoke gather along the ceiling, Dwayne grabbed the chain between his feet and jerked it.

"The keys," he said. "You have to get me out of here."

The boy looked uncertainly at Dwayne's cuffed ankles and wrinkled his nose. "Why should I?" he said. "Why should I unlock you when you didn't unlock us?"

And how exactly was Dwayne supposed to respond to that? The kid was right, of course.

"Please," he said, "I'm sorry. I didn't want this." That was the truth, no matter how it might have looked to the kid. Dwayne had been too weak to beat his addiction, but he'd never dreamed he'd find himself in a position like this. How could he? No one could have foreseen this nightmare. "Please don't let me die here."

Something in the boy's face softened. Dwayne saw a kind of innocence there, what he hoped might even be forgiveness of a sort. "I have to get the other kids first."

Dwayne nodded. Of course. Monstrous as it might have been, even if for just a moment, he'd forgotten about the other kids.

"Same keys." He coughed. The room was half full of smoke now. "They're on a ring on a peg by the door downstairs." He nodded his head toward the basement stairs, just visible through the kitchen doorway. He'd only been down there once, and once had been enough. "You can get them out and then come back for me, yeah?"

The kid looked him up and down and said only, "I'll be back." He ran to the stairs, hurried down, and was gone.

Dwayne dropped to the floor, noticed for the first time how warm the surface had become, and tugged again at the chain between his feet. On the television, Mulder dove into the backseat of a car and motioned for Scully to go.

Yes, go, Dwayne thought at her. *Get the hell out of there!*

He coughed into a fist, wiped sweat and tears from the corners of his eyes. Why were there no smoke alarms? No approaching fire engines? He heard only the invisible storm outside and an intensifying crackling below.

That's Hell. This time the voice in his head wasn't his own. *The devil's got your number, and he's calling.*

When the boy returned, it was at the head of a group of crying, red-eyed children. One of the bigger boys carried a slim red-haired girl over his shoulder, looking like a miniature fireman. The kids didn't push past each other the way Dwayne might have expected but filed quickly and carefully into the room.

Dwayne motioned Bucket Feet over. "Okay," he said. "Now get me out of here. Please."

The big boy repositioned the girl on his shoulder and shook his head. "Don't do it. It's a trick."

"No trick." Dwayne shook his head. "Please."

Bucket Feet sucked his bottom lip, looked from Dwayne to the keys in his hand.

"Please." The sounds of rattling chains seemed to come not only from between his feet now but from everywhere, both inside the house and out.

The kid let out a long breath, gave Dwayne the faintest hint of a nod, and took a step in his direction, but before he could move any closer, a door at the end of the back hall flew open and slapped the wall.

The pharmacist stood in the doorway, a gun in one hand, a loop of chain in the other, and a look of incredulity on his bloody, beaten face. Cold air and splattering sleet blew in around him.

Several of the children screamed. Dwayne only watched. Watched the gun come up. Watched the pharmacist's finger squeeze the trigger. Watched the muzzle flash. Felt a sudden pressure on one side of his neck and then a strange emptiness on the other.

As some liquid—*my blood*, he thought, *this is my blood*—began to pool around his head, he saw the pharmacist point the gun at the children. Instead of firing again, however, he lowered the weapon, backed up smiling, and closed the door. Dwayne heard a familiar sound then, a sound he'd lived with for what seemed an eternity. The clinking, rattling, and clanging lasted only a few seconds, but it didn't take longer than that for the realization to sink in. The pharmacist had chained the door shut. With Dwayne inside. With the children inside. With the fire inside.

Not that it mattered much to Dwayne anymore. As the pool around his head grew, the world around him shrank.

And the last strange thing Dwayne saw in his too-short life was his own body, lying lifeless on a dirty kitchen floor near a crowd of sobbing children while his spirit drifted down through the floor and into the blazing inferno below.

The trunk shrank with each passing second. Although she'd never been particularly claustrophobic, Addie had long since lost any kind of grip she might once have had on her composure. Every muscle in her face clenched. Her arms and legs trembled. If she didn't get out soon, she feared her mind might shut down and never re-open.

The girl lay beside her, a small fist gripping Addie's shirt just above the hip.

Addie pressed her hand against the trunk's cool lid, wanting to punch it, scratch it, claw her way through it, and knowing she could do none of those things, could only touch it and let it leech out the last of her warmth.

The car rolled over a bump and Addie licked her bloody lips.

Clutching tighter still, the little fist pinched a handful of Addie's skin in a way that was mildly painful and fiercely invigorating.

She had to hold it together. For the girl's sake if not her own.

Shelly. Her name is Shelly.

Yes. That was right. Another Shelly. Which surprised her not at all.

Still trembling but doing her best to sound like a comforting, balanced adult, she wrapped an arm around the little girl and told her everything would be okay.

"Those were the train tracks."

Addie inhaled. Squeezed her eyes shut. Exhaled.

"We're almost there."

"Where?" Addie opened her eyes. Or thought she did. She could no longer tell.

"The Hole."

"What does that mean?"

Shelly wiggled closer and rested her head on Addie's shoulder. "We're almost there," she said again. As if that explained everything.

The car slid around a corner, and for a moment it seemed the trunk had been custom made to magnify the sensation: spinning tires slipping liquidly across the roadway, slush splattering and thumping against the twisting axels. Each sound and motion traveled up through the undercarriage, reverberating through the trunk's frame and into their huddled bodies.

When the car slowed, Shelly pressed closer still, practically melding her body into Addie's, and by the time they skated to a complete stop, they were quaking in sync.

"We're here," Shelly said.

The fresh tears running down Addie's cheek could have belonged to anyone.

"There!" Bugs pointed to a cluster of bunnies only he could see.

As Gladys spun the wheel, she gave Bugs a quick, worried look. He saw a million questions tucked behind her pursed lips, but she said nothing. This kind of acquiescence was something Bugs had rarely come across, and he couldn't have been happier about it—the fewer questions she asked, the less he had to lie—but he couldn't sit here in her borrowed coat and homemade hat and say nothing, couldn't let her put her life on the line (and there was absolutely no question that she *was* doing that) without so much as a thank you.

"You're a lifesaver," he said.

She laughed.

"Is that funny?"

"It is." She tapped the brakes as they slid across an icy patch of road. "I helped my daddy when I was a girl and he was choking on a lump of sausage. They didn't have that Heimlich thingy back then, but I pounded his back until he hawked it up. He used to call me Little Lifesaver. Like a nickname. You remind me of him."

Bugs thought of Granny Ilene again and told her maybe they'd been related in a previous life.

"Could be," she said. "If you believe in that kind of thing."

"Do you?"

The wipers flapped furiously across the windshield, brushing away layer after layer of fresh snow.

Gladys nodded. "Actually, I do. Ghosts, miracles, Bigfoot, aliens. My kids call me silly, but I believe in just about everything. Never had a reason not to."

Bugs would never say he believed in *everything*, but after all the things he'd seen, he guessed his mind was more open than most. He liked Gladys. Despite everything, it felt good to share some time with a kindred spirit.

He just hoped he didn't get this particular spirit in trouble.

"I don't think you're silly," he said.

She thanked him, and the genuine gratitude in her voice left him with an equally genuine lump in his throat.

"Your wife," Gladys said, and any temporary sense of comfort Bugs might have felt slid away like so much windshield mush. "What kind of trouble is she in?"

Bugs swallowed his lump. "The worst kind," he said. And because he sensed he could trust her with at least some of the truth, he added, "She's been taken."

"Taken?"

Bugs left out most of the details, including the dead patrolman, but he told her about Tirechanger, about the girl with duct tape on her mouth, about the other children, and of course about the altercation that ended with Addie in the trunk.

He spun his wedding ring.

Gladys turned to him for an uncomfortably—dangerously—long moment. "We have to call the authorities."

Watching the road, ready to scream if the truck drifted or the road curved, Bugs said, "Definitely. As soon as we can. But there's something else."

"What else?" She re-focused on the job of driving, and Bugs breathed again.

He told her what the girl had said about the local police.

"That doesn't matter," she said.

"It doesn't?"

"No." She wiped at a patch of windshield that had started to fog. "We've got something better than cops."

Sensing she wouldn't continue until he asked her what that something might be, Bugs obliged.

"My son," she said, and you couldn't have mistaken the look on her face for anything but absolute pride. "He's an FBI bigwig. He hates when I say it that way, but that's what he is. And they have a field office not thirty miles from here."

Bugs laughed. Maybe the fact that he could still laugh in a situation like this should have surprised him, but it didn't. Of course her son was an FBI bigwig. And nearby at that. It was the kind of thing that happened to him all the time. Luck. Fate. Whatever. He'd taken it for granted most of his life.

"No wonder they led me to you."

She looked at him again, but only briefly this time. "Who?"

Bugs shook his head. "My guardian angels, I guess." It wasn't what the rabbits were—not exactly—but he hoped it would satisfy her.

It did.

A new group of rabbits shuffled through the snow beside the road ahead. Half a dozen this time. He directed her to take the next turn. They passed houses and buildings on both sides, all nearly lost in the snowstorm.

"So what are we doing?" she asked. "Where are we going? How do you know where to go?"

Bugs blew out a long breath. Here came the questions after all, and he didn't blame her a bit for asking them. But he also knew he couldn't get into it. Not only because he didn't know what to say, but because he sensed they were closing in on the car, maybe only minutes away now.

"We aren't doing anything," he said. "Once we've caught up to them, you're going to let me out and keep right on going. Get to a phone. Call your son. Send help."

"Bull hockey." She wiped at the window again and returned her knuckly fingers to the wheel. "What kind of guardian angel would that make me?"

Although Bugs had never called *her* a guardian angel, he supposed she was. As much as the rabbits anyway, if not more so. He said, "The breathing kind," and she harumphed.

Ahead, Bugs spied the snow-covered remains of what might have been a gas station once upon a time. A FOR SALE sign dangled beneath a corrugated canopy out front. The chain on one side of the sign had come loose from the canopy and dragged the bare concrete where the snow hadn't quite reached as the cockeyed sign blew in the wind.

Another fluffle of rabbits stood in the road ahead, urging him on, telling him to *hurry*. One particularly large specimen stood on its hind legs in the center of the group, long ears flapping in the wind, nose twitching. The truck's headlights illuminated the creature as they ran it through.

Hold on, Addie. I'm coming.

Gladys slowed as they approached a railroad crossing. The road humped where the tracks crossed it. Bugs spied the ice-encrusted warning lights and the inactive railroad gate pointing up into the night sky, but just barely. If the storm intensified much more, they'd be dealing with a full-on white-out.

The truck bounced over the tracks and rolled on. More rabbits appeared on the other side. A few at first. Then more. Then MORE. Dozens of the animals skittered frantically around the side of the road ahead. In this weather, Bugs never would have noticed the turn on his own. Other than a wider-than-usual gap between some trees, the area looked no different from any of the other surroundings.

"Here!" he said. "Turn here."

Gladys slowed. "I don't think there's anywhere *to* turn," she said, "I—"

"No, look. See the tracks?"

You could only barely make them out. Although it couldn't have been more than a few minutes since Tirechanger passed through, the storm had already done its level best to fill the ruts. But they were there, no doubt about it. And, of course, Bugs didn't need to see them at all to know which way to go.

Gladys squinted, nodded, and slowed the truck to a crawl before turning into the gap and proceeding.

The wipers squeaked across the cold, fogged glass. More rabbits lined the road ahead. They didn't exactly form an arrow, but they might as well have.

And then Bugs saw it. Already covered with a dusting of snow, angled in front of a ranch-style house that was almost entirely obscured by the snowfall: Tirechanger's car.

Four rabbits sat on the trunk. Watching him with their glowing, headlit eyes. Waiting.

"Stop here."

She slid the truck to a stop several car lengths from the other vehicle.

Trees and bushes surrounded the property. Bugs could see them—or the vague, shadow-lump versions of them anyway—but nothing beyond. If there were neighbors, they were hidden in the snowfall.

A series of small craters pocked the snow around the car and led toward the house. Tirechanger's footprints, he assumed. But had he taken Addie and the girl with him? Bugs didn't know. And he *hated* not knowing. He'd spent much of his life rushing blindly into dangerous situations, forging ahead with nothing but a sliver of hope, but he'd never gotten used to it. Not really.

"You have to go now," Bugs said. "Call your son."

She shook her head. "I'm staying until it's done. Period." The unwavering command in that last word precluded any further debate.

He asked if she had any tools with her. A crowbar. A hammer. Anything like that.

She tilted her head toward the truck bed. "There's a tire iron in the spare kit. Why?"

Another tire iron. Of course.

"Get it," he said, "and wait here."

He took off her coat and hat and offered them back to her.

"You need those."

"So do you," Bugs said. "If you're staying, you're taking them back." Now it was his turn to be adamant. "I'll be okay for a few minutes." He dropped the garments on the seat between them.

"I'll take the coat. You take the hat." She picked up the knit cap and tossed it in his lap.

Bugs didn't want to argue any further. Addie was here. Maybe hurt. Certainly scared. He'd never wanted anything more in life than to hold her in his arms.

And the girl too, of course. Shelly. His mission. Or part of it anyway. He hadn't forgotten her.

He tugged the butterfly cap down over his ears, wincing when it brushed against the pair of throbbing lumps Tirechanger had given him all those thousands of years ago. He gave his new Little Lifesaver what he hoped was a reassuring look and stepped out into the storm.

The cold hit him like an avalanche. He tucked his head and turned his back to the gusting wind. It took what felt like an impossible amount of willpower not to dive immediately back into the truck's heavenly warmth.

Instead, he shut his door and trudged through the deepening snow as fast as his worn muscles and unseasonable sneakers would carry him. The truck's headlights lit the scene, reflecting off the pelting snow. His shadow stretched out from the spot where his shins met the snow and on into infinity. He watched the car as he moved, trying to blink the snow out of his eyes, feeling it already thickening his lashes and brows. He didn't think Tirechanger would pop up from behind the vehicle, but if he'd kept a rulebook, rule #1 definitely would have been to expect the unexpected.

At the car, he cupped his hands over the sides of his face and leaned close to the icy windows.

Nothing inside but the wads of duct tape he and Addie had removed earlier and the loops of jumper cables he'd once hinged all their hopes on peeking out from beneath the front seat.

"Addie?" He didn't bother whispering. The wind was blowing from the direction of the house. Anyone more than a few feet away would have heard nothing but the wet, whooshing sounds of the storm.

The trunk thumped. Addie said something, but the word was muffled, unintelligible.

"I'm here!" he said, grinning and swallowing blizzard.

When he tried the handle on the driver's door, the door popped open with an icy crunch.

Good. They wouldn't need Gladys's tire iron after all.

He reached inside and pulled the trunk's release lever with one freezing hand.

Something mechanical unlatched—he could tell that much—but unlike the driver's door, the trunk didn't pop open.

Stuck.

He shuffled to the rear of the car, glancing back at the

truck and making a come-on motion he hoped Gladys could see.

The popsicles jutting from his palms poked at the trunk, but he could no longer make them curl.

He leaned close to the trunk and yelled, "Push."

The lid wriggled for a second before flying open, sending sheets of ice and snow flying in every direction.

Beneath it, Addie and Shelly lay curled in each other's arms. Addie's lips were bloody, and they'd both clearly been crying, but for the most part, they looked okay. They were alive anyway, and that was half the battle.

Addie sat up, pulling the girl with her, and Bugs leaned in to give them both the strongest, purest, most necessary hug he'd ever given.

"We're okay." He and Addie said it at the exact same time, and then they laughed.

Bugs heard crunching sounds behind him, pulled out of the hug, and spun around ready to fight. But it was only Gladys, carrying a long metal item with one hand and clutching her coat to herself with the other.

"Who..." Addie started and shook her head. "Never mind. Introductions later. Shelly says this is the place he keeps some of the kids."

The little girl nodded. Her thin pajamas blew in the wind. Clothing had never looked so insubstantial.

"Victor," she said. "And the other kids."

"Someone took you?" Gladys said. "And other kids? And they're all here?"

Bugs had already explained that part of it, but he didn't blame her for wanting to verify the information.

She only had bits and pieces of the whole story. Honestly, he couldn't believe she'd gone along this far.

"Yes," Shelly said. "No. Not all of them. Only some. And my brother."

"If there are kids in there, we need to go now," Gladys said and gestured into the sky above the house.

"I don't—" But then he saw what she meant. You could barely make it out through the storm, but curls of smoke rose from multiple spots on the roof. And none of those spots were chimneys. An odd glow seeped from gaps around what appeared to be boarded-over windows.

The house was on fire.

"You have to get these two out of here," he told Gladys. "Take the truck. Make your call. I'll take care of things here."

Two women and one girl shook their heads at him in exact syncopation, and he realized he was hopelessly outnumbered.

"We stick together," Addie said.

And now their shakes became nods. Again, exactly in sync.

Bugs sighed and said they better get going then. He helped Addie out of the trunk and picked up Shelly.

"Let me have her," Gladys said. "I can fit her under my coat."

"She won't be too heavy?"

Gladys tilted her head and frowned. "I'm not useless," she said. "I can carry one little wisp of a girl."

And Bugs believed she could.

Once they'd gotten Shelly tucked successfully (if

somewhat awkwardly) against the old woman's chest, the group moved.

The land sloped upward. Between the incline and the wind blowing in their faces, their progress was agonizingly slow. They followed Tirechanger's still-visible tracks. Addie led the pack, and Bugs followed only steps behind. He never wanted to let her out of his sight again. Gladys brought up the rear.

When they reached the house, Bugs could feel the heat emanating off it, despite the storm and his bone-deep chill.

Only a few steps later, he heard a grunt and a rustling behind him and turned to see Shelly wriggling out of Gladys's grasp.

"No," Gladys said, either because she'd lost control of the child or herself. She plopped back into the snow on her bottom.

Shelly bolted away, running toward and then past Bugs and Addie.

"Victor!"

Bugs reached for her but...you know...popsicles.

Addie also grabbed at the child, also unsuccessfully.

They ran after her as best they could, but where they sank into the snow, Shelly seemed to run across the surface, as if she weighed nothing, her little carrot socks gathering snow but never fully disappearing.

"STOP!" Bugs yelled after her, but she didn't. Maybe she could no longer hear him. Maybe she just didn't want to listen.

He looked back to make sure Gladys was okay, but she was no longer sitting in the snow. She wasn't there at all.

"GLADYS!"

No response.

Great. Now what? Did he go after the girl or the granny?

He looked left. Looked right. A rabbit appeared in the direction Shelly had run, standing on the snow between him and Addie.

He took Addie's hand as best he could and they hurried along the house that way, kicking at the snow, pulling each other forward when one of their feet sank especially deep.

Bugs thought he saw a shape in the distance that might have been another structure. Not a house, but maybe a shed or a small garage. It disappeared behind a fresh swirl of snow.

Shelly ran around the house's back corner.

"Shelly!" Addie yelled, and Bugs heard the grief in her voice.

Bugs pumped his legs with every last bit of strength he had. He could no longer feel his feet.

They finally scrambled around the corner themselves. And into the worst possible situation...

"Well looky what we have here," Tirechanger said. He stood near the back door with Shelly in one arm, squeezing her against his chest, face out. He had a gun to her head.

Bugs started forward, but Addie pulled him back.

"Put her down," Bugs said. He wasn't sure he'd ever heard such uncontrolled rage in his own voice.

"Nah," Tirechanger said. "She's always been more trouble than she's worth." His swollen nose had gotten worse—the words came out in a drone.

"I had big plans tonight," he said. "You know that? Before you two assholes came along and ruined everything." He pressed the gun's muzzle tight against Shelly's temple.

Bugs shook with cold and anger, an earthquake in the shape of a man.

"How did you get here?" Tirechanger asked Bugs and looked suddenly, genuinely confused.

Bugs said nothing.

Loops of chain encircled the back door's handle. Bugs noticed this with a kind of detached curiosity.

"Never mind. Doesn't matter. We'll just make a new plan, right? That's one thing the world will never run out of." He laughed.

Bugs could say with one hundred percent certainty that he'd never been more disconcerted.

Shelly kicked at the maniac's legs, but he didn't appear phased and didn't loosen his grip.

"He's in there," Shelly said and looked toward the house. "Victor!"

"He was," Tirechanger said. "True true. But they—"

The sound that cut him off might have been an axe striking a tree stump. Or a home run in some Frankenstein sport where you hit a football with a baseball bat.

Tirechanger dropped Shelly. She fell face first in the snow with a wet *whomp*.

Still pointing the gun at the empty spot where the girl's head had been, Tirechanger stood motionless for one long second, his eyes wide. Then those same eyes—those wild, mad eyes—rolled into the back of his head and he fell too. If you could call such an unnatural, sideways flop a fall. His body slapped the snow and lay there motionless.

Behind where he'd been standing, Gladys stood with the tire iron still raised over her shoulder. "Bet you didn't plan on that."

Bugs let out a sound that was half laugh, half scream, and all disbelief.

She must have circled the house, come upon him from behind. Although why she'd thought to do such a thing, Bugs had no idea.

Gladys knelt beside Tirechanger and pulled the tire iron back as if to strike again.

"NO!" Bugs screamed.

Gladys looked at him, and he shook his head. "Don't kill him. If you haven't already. There are more kids, and he needs to tell us where. Or tell your son anyway."

"The kids," Addie said and ran for the back door. Shelly had pulled herself up and beat her there. The two of them tugged uselessly at the chained handle. At their feet, three rabbits stood on their hind legs, pawing at the door.

Bugs schlepped over to Tirechanger, checked his pockets. He found a phone, a wad of cash, and a keyring. The gun lay in the snow beside him.

He handed the phone and the gun to Gladys, told her to make her call and watch Tirechanger, and hurried to the door with the keys.

The chain looped around the door handle and a steel ring in the frame multiple times. A heavy-duty padlock secured it. There must have been thirty keys on the ring. In a movie, he might have gone through them all before finding the one that unlocked this particular lock, but this wasn't a movie, and his old buddy Luck was there for him once again—the second key he tried did the trick. The lock fell to the snow, and Addie jerked the chain free.

Bugs felt the handle. It was only slightly warm.

When he opened the door, a plume of smoke blew through the opening. In the hallway beyond, he saw the pile of bodies.

"Oh my god." Addie's hand slipped over her mouth.

"Victor!" Shelly ran into the house and Bugs went after her.

She stopped beside a small, ashy boy and grabbed his arm. "Wake up," she said and coughed. "Victor, wake up."

Bugs picked up the boy and carried him out into the snow. Addie had gone in behind him. She dragged out a big beast of a kid who must have weighed nearly as much as she did.

Between the two of them, they managed to get all eight children out of the house. There was one more person inside, but he was beyond help.

Out in the snow, some of the children stirred, coughed, vomited. Two of them didn't.

Bugs's eyes stung from the smoke. His mouth tasted like charcoal. He knelt beside one of the moving kids, a very young girl with a mess of red hair. "Is this everyone?"

The girl looked around, as if unsure of where she was.

Bugs grabbed her shoulder, carefully, and looked directly into her eyes. "You're okay," he said. "We're here to help you, but I need to know if this is everyone. How many kids were inside?"

She held up one hand with all five fingers showing and another with only three.

"Eight?" Bugs said. "There are eight of you?"

She nodded. Then she began to cry.

"It's okay," he repeated. "You'll be okay."

Gladys stood nearby, relaying information into the kidnapper's phone. Addie knelt beside one of the still children, the absolute unit she'd dragged out first. "He's breathing," she said.

Bugs shuffled over to Shelly and the barefoot boy he assumed must be her brother.

"Please," she wailed. Her face was awash with tears. "Help him."

Bugs dropped to his knees beside the child, pressed his ear against the small chest and felt for air coming out of the soot-covered nostrils.

Nothing.

"Move back," he said, but Shelly didn't. She clutched her brother's hand and continued bawling.

Bugs tilted the boy's head back, pinched his nose, and blew two breaths into his mouth. After just barely saving a drowning woman years earlier, he and Addie had taken a CPR course together. Since then, he'd performed the procedure more times than he cared to count, but never on a child.

Never until now.

When the boy didn't respond, he began chest compressions, counting out loud.

He only got to ten.

Victor wheezed, opened his eyes, and barfed out a puddle of gray bile. Bugs turned him on his side, told him he'd be okay now, and gently patted his back, helping him bring up another mouthful of vomit.

Shelly wrapped her arms around the boy's body, getting some of his mess on her hands and not seeming to care a bit.

Gladys, who appeared to have finished her call, approached smiling. "Who's the Little Lifesaver now?" she said.

He slumped back in the snow.

"Help's on the way. It'll take some time in this weather, but they'll get here."

Bugs nodded and let out what felt like six lungs' worth of air. The exhalation floated around his face and drifted up into the storm.

A hand gripped his shoulder. When he looked up, he saw Addie's face hovering above.

"We need to get them out of the cold," she said.

"A garage," Bugs said. "Or a shed." He nodded toward the far end of the back yard. He'd never been so cold in his life. Not even close. "I saw something back there."

While Addie and Gladys ushered the kids across the snow-covered lawn, Bugs curled his elbows under Tirechanger's armpits and dragged him in the same direction. They used the chain from the back door to secure him to a post in what turned out to be a fairly large garage. Just in case, Bugs removed the maniac's shoelaces and tied those around his wrists too. He thought he might have cut off the man's circulation and didn't feel an iota of guilt.

The children huddled on the other side of the room. Addie had found some old moth-eaten blankets and a tarp to drape over them. None of them said a word. Bugs didn't know how you could ever overcome something like this, but kids could be surprisingly resilient.

Please let them be okay. Alive is great, but alive and okay is even better.

He tried not to think about how tonight could have turned out. If the rabbits hadn't led him here, if he and Addie hadn't knocked Tirechanger off whatever sinister course he'd been on, those eight little souls would be gone. Burned alive. And who knew where Shelly might be. Or what might be happening to her.

He slapped the sides of his face, tried to knock the thoughts right out of his head.

Then, after checking Tirechanger's restraints for what must have been the tenth time, he pulled Gladys to the side.

"We did good, didn't we?"

Bugs nodded and told her they'd done *great*. "But there's one more thing I need you to do."

Gladys waited.

"They're going to ask how we found them," Bugs said.

Before he could go on, Gladys nodded. "And you need me to lie." It wasn't a question.

Bugs thought she might lie for him, even to her own son, but he had no intention of asking her to do that. "Not lie," he said, "but just tell a version of the truth that doesn't lead to questions I can't answer."

"And what version would that be?"

So Bugs laid it out. Tirechanger had taken Addie and left him. Gladys, she of life saving fame, had found Bugs alone on the road and picked him up, and then they'd followed Tirechanger here. All true, technically. Unless someone asked how closely they'd followed, they'd never have to tell an outright lie.

"Okay," Gladys said. "I can do that. On one condition."

"What's that?"

"You tell me what really happened."

Bugs smiled and assured her he would. Every bit of it. And he meant it. But not until after.

"We'll have you over for dinner," he said, "and I'll tell you everything you want to know. I don't know if you'll believe it all, and I don't fully understand it all myself, but I'll tell you."

They shook on it. Her skin was calloused, liver spotted, and wrinkled, and it was the most pleasant shake of his life.

A few minutes later, Bugs felt a tug on his pants. Most of the feeling had come back into his legs, although his fingers still wouldn't bend.

Shelly stood beside him, chewing her lower lip.

"Hey," he said, "how's your brother?"

Gnawing away at that poor little lip, the girl nodded. "Okay, I think."

Bugs knelt, trying to get closer to her level. Before he could steady himself, she threw her arms around his neck and pulled herself against him.

"Thank you," she said. "Thank you for saving us."

Bugs hugged her back. "You're welcome."

When she let him go, he put a reassuring hand on the top of her head.

"Are we really going to be okay now?"

Bugs nodded. "Safe and sound. We'll get you back..." And just then, he remembered something she'd said earlier, something about her and her brother being different. He asked her what she'd meant by that.

She looked toward the still-unconscious kidnapper, and Bugs had a sudden, terrible thought.

"He's not your...dad, is he?"

Shelly wrinkled her nose. "Eww. No. That's gross."

He couldn't help but chuckle at that.

"So what makes you two different? If you don't mind telling me."

She hesitated briefly before saying, "We went with him on purpose."

Bugs frowned. "On purpose?"

"We ran away from home. It was just a game. We were going to go back for dinner. But we got lost." She chewed her lip again. "He told us he would drive us home. I know you're not supposed to go with strangers, but I was stupid."

"No," Bugs said. "No no. You weren't stupid."

Taking a ride from a stranger *was* a mistake, of course, but she didn't need him to tell her that now.

Shelly nodded. "It was all my fault." Tears slipped down her cheeks.

Bugs hugged her again. "This was not your fault," he whispered. "Never think that, okay?"

He pulled away, holding her at arm's length. "That's a

bad man over there, and every bad thing that happened was his fault. Only his. Okay?"

Shelly nodded. "Okay."

Bugs could only hope she believed it.

She smiled at him and went back to her brother, who made room for her under the blanket and rested his head on her shoulder.

Bugs found Addie, and the two of them stood at a window that wasn't completely frosted over. While they waited for the authorities, Addie wrapped her arm around his waist.

"Nice hat," she said.

He reached up. He'd forgotten all about Gladys's hat. "Pretty cunning, don't you think?"

She laughed and gave the brim a tug. "Are they gone?"

And, of course, he didn't have to ask what she meant by that.

Putting his own arm around her shoulders, Bugs nodded. "Mission accomplished."

They stood that way, warming each other and talking quietly, until they saw the flashing lights in the distance.

EPILOGUE

As the garage door rolled down behind them, Bugs leaned back in the driver's seat, closed his eyes, and sighed.

"I never want to give another statement as long as I live."

Addie put a hand on his thigh. "Dream on."

Bugs shut off the engine and made a pair of fists, easing the fingers inward. They were stiff and painful but working. The paramedics had cleaned the wounds on his head and found no signs of permanent damage there or anywhere else.

Lucky, they'd said.

When you had a head full of rabbits' feet, how could you *not* be?

In the console between them, his phone buzzed.

He flipped it around and looked at the screen. Shelly.

And, of course, he couldn't help but think of the little girl who shared this woman's name. Where was she now? Still stuck somewhere in a cheap administrative

Safe and sound in her own little bed?

Probably not. Not yet. But soon.

One of the worst things about his life was that he often lost track of the people he'd helped. There were news stories, of course, and the occasional call or text or even letter, but usually he never heard from them again. And that made sense, he knew. Even if they remembered him with love, thought of him as the man who'd plucked them from disaster, the haunting memory of that disaster was still there too. You couldn't remember the man who'd saved you without also remembering what he'd saved you *from*. It was a bummer, and a burden, but he'd learned to live with it.

He tapped the phone. The text from Shelly showed a sleek, sporty wheel chair.

"Check out the new wheels!" the message below it read.

He showed the picture to Addie.

"Tell her she should paint flames down the sides."

He did, and they both smiled when she sent back a devil emoji.

He would call her later, but right now, he wanted to crawl into a steaming shower and stay there until he grew gills.

When they entered the kitchen, Bugs spotted the half-eaten turkey sandwiches on the table in the breakfast nook.

His stomach growled.

He hurried to the table and wolfed down his unfinished dinner in three barely chewed bites.

"That's nasty," Addie said. "Those have been sitting

out since yesterday."

Had it been yesterday? He looked at the microwave clock. Yes, technically.

A few specks of dust floated in the glass of water beside his plate, but he didn't care. He gulped it down.

"Does that mean I can have yours?"

She rolled her eyes and made a go-head gesture.

As he finished the meal she'd been halfway through when the first rabbit appeared, she grabbed something fresh for herself from the fridge.

She wanted a bath, so she took the guest bathroom and he took the master. He stood beneath the spray and scrubbed the smorgasbord of muck from his body: blood, soot, grime, sweat. He stood there until the water finally ran clear, and then he stood there longer. When he got tired of standing, he sat, letting the hot spray sluice across every inch of his pruning skin. It must have been at least an hour before he finally called it quits. By then, he felt almost clean, almost refreshed, almost normal.

The bedroom beckoned. He could feel the cool, soft pillow beneath his head, the pile of thick blankets across his body, Addie behind him, big spoon to his little. But first, he swallowed a handful of aspirin and brushed his teeth.

His reflection watched him from the mirror, its baggy eyes telling him to get some rest. Begging him.

Thank you for saving us. It was a voice he thought

might occupy his mind for some time to come. Maybe forever. He pictured the little carrot socks, the siblings huddled together beneath the moth-eaten blanket.

"You're welcome," he said and rinsed the toothpaste from his lips.

In the bedroom, he slipped into a pair of pajama pants and called for Addie.

No response.

He turned toward the bed and stopped.

A rabbit sat on the comforter, its nose twitching, its long, perky ears pointed up toward the ceiling. He could see the headboard through its shimmering torso.

It sat on Addie's pillow.

No.

He yelled for her again.

Nothing.

He pictured her in the bathroom, a lump on her head where she'd slipped and hit the edge of the tub, her lifeless eyes pointing up at him from beneath the surface of the water.

And then he pictured Tirechanger, standing over a tub of pinkening water, a straight razor in his hand and a maniacal grin on his face.

No.

He ran to the bathroom and yanked open the door.

Addie lay with her head on the bath pillow, eyes closed, listening to something on her earbuds and bobbing her head slowly to the music.

Bugs knelt and touched her shoulder.

She jerked, screeched, and splashed sudsy, lilac-scented water onto the floor.

Bugs scooted out of the puddle and said, "Are you okay?"

She took the earbuds out, and he repeated the question.

"I'm fine," she said. "What's..." She groaned. "You saw another one, didn't you?"

He rubbed his temples and nodded. "But I can deal with it this time. You stay here."

She shook her head, got out of the tub, and wrapped a towel around herself. "That's not the deal."

"I know, but—"

She shushed him. "You get the keys. I'll get the coats."

They got dressed, crawled back into the car, and pulled away from the house. As Addie activated the headlights and wipers, Bugs cranked the heater.

"Which way?" she said.

Bugs scanned the snowy landscape, looking for the next sign, and pointed.

A NOTE FROM THE AUTHOR

I think I need to tell you why this book exists.

It all starts with care packages. You know about care packages, right? Boxes of snacks and cash and...I don't know...condoms? Parents love to send them—homesick college students love to receive them. Well, twenty-some years ago, a devilishly handsome college sophomore thought it would be funny to buck the trend and send a care package of his own back home to his mom. Why did he decide this? Was he drunk on the moonshine he and his fellow classmates fermented in the broken washing machine in the first floor laundry room? No! That's slander! Stop slandering him!

But seriously, I was.

I mean he was.

Okay, fine, he was me and I was he and we were both the walrus, and maybe I'm a little drunk on moonshine right now. You'll never know.

But you should know this: I have no idea what I put in that package. Seriously. No recollection whatsoever.

Except for one thing...

First, however, you need to know that my mom loves rabbits. Has since she was a little girl. I don't know what about them intrigues her, and I'm not sure she knows herself, but for as long as I can remember, it's been one of life's most incontrovertible truths: my mom loves rabbits.

Back then, I had written four novels (my four unpublishable practice novels, as I think of them now) and many short stories. My mom had always been incredibly supportive of my writing, and I knew if I was going to send home a care package, it needed to include one thing for sure: a bunny story.

So I wrote one. A science fiction story about a man stranded on an alien planet with an android and, you guessed it, some rabbits.

I dropped the story in a box along with a few other things I thought she might like, and away it went.

That first story was just for fun, but after that, it became a thing. Every year for Mother's Day and her birthday, I'd write a new bunny story. I think I might have missed a few holidays over the years, but not many. At some point along the way, I had an idea for something longer. How much longer? I didn't know then. But I knew I'd have to break it up and write her two new parts each year until it was done. As it turns out, I needed sixteen chapters to tell the whole story, and it took me the better part of a decade. (I know what you math wizzes are thinking, but I already told you I might have missed a few holidays, okay?)

The book you hold now is that story. I wrote it for my mom, and I never intended for anyone else in the world to see it, but once it was done, I thought some of the rest of you might get a kick out of it.

I hope you did.

Daniel Pyle
May 1, 2022

ACKNOWLEDGEMENTS

There are usually many people involved in the production of a book, and with all my other work, I've had help from scores of kind, smart, wonderful individuals, but this project has been different. Because it was so personal, I wanted to do as much as possible myself. Cover design: check. Formatting: yep. Editing: I did my best. Bearing so much of the brunt is undoubtedly a stupid thing to do, but in this case, it felt like the *right* stupid thing, for better or worse.

But no man is an island, even when he wants to be, and there are a few people I need to thank for their help with this labor of love.

First, Robert Duperre, a man whose writing I admire and whose opinion I respect immensely. Thank you for your feedback and your friendship.

Then there's Amy Pyle, my marvelous wife, the Addie to my Bugs. She stood by me every step of the way, offering sage advice, encouragement, and help. I'm so glad we're in this together.

And, of course, my mom, who's been there for me since the age of negative nine months. Great moms inspire curiosity, nurture creativity, and teach us that as long as we try our best, there's always at least one person out there who's proud of us. My mom did all of that and so much more, and I can never thank her enough. I love you, Freakin Mom.